D0559175

The Canine Connection

contents

The Canine Connection

lab

I'VE GOT THIS GREAT IDEA for a story about a laboratory where they experiment on Labrador retrievers, so the title is "Lab"—what my dad would call a double entendre, meaning two things at once—but unfortunately I don't ever get very far past the title. Every time I read about laboratories where they experiment on dogs, I get sick to my stomach. It doesn't bother me to read science books. I do that all the time, plus volunteering at the vet's, but veterinarians try to *help* animals. Anyway, the main character in this story is a kid named Will who gets a job in one of these labs and he's all excited because he wants to win a Nobel

Prize for research someday, but then he gets attached to one of the dogs and it dies while they're doing surgery on it and he goes ballistic. You can see the point I'm trying to make here about labs and Labs but, like my dad says, the devil is in the details and I can't stomach the details of this story. I just want to make the point. My mother thinks that's my biggest problem, but she makes a lot of points herself.

We've never gotten along too well, my mother and I. My dad says it's because we're so much alike—okay, we're both female—and I'm the oldest, so she and I butt heads while the rest of the kids go their merry ways and do whatever they want. That's another problem, there are too many kids in this family. It's like my parents never heard of zero population growth. They claim to have wanted each and every one of us. There are a lot of unwanted kids in the world, I point out, and they could have adopted a couple of them. Then where would you be, asks my mother. She's pretty smart for a plain ordinary housewife. You don't see too many of those anymore. They're like an endangered species. So treat her carefully, says my dad. On the other hand if she hadn't had five kids she could have taught school or run an orphanage or been the boss of something else besides us. She even bosses my dad. "Blessed are the meek for they shall inherit the earth," says my dad, quoting the Bible, of course, which he does all the time, being a minister. My dad has earned a lot of earth. "Blessed are the peacemakers," blessed is this, blessed is that.

I seem to specialize in the unblessed. Or as my mother would say, the unwanted and the abnormal. And I say right back to her, you'd be abnormal too if you were unwanted. She glares at me and then at my black Labrador retriever, Sinbad, who was named by my father after Sinbad the sailor because Labs love water but also because Sinbad sins badly. Another one of those double entendres. Sinbad was a science laboratory reject, according to his previous three owners. I don't know what they did to him in that lab, or planned to do to him, but one thing is clear, he was never what dog people would call socialized. This is a hyperactive dog that eats not just shoes but also sofas and forgets commands before he learns them and pays no attention to human beings. The only creature he has ever responded to is a white duck named Lucy that one of my sisters won at an Easter egg hunt. Talk about unchristian—it's thoughtless and cruel, handing out live animals as prizes. Some people would probably have just eaten the duck for dinner but this duck was lucky. We gave her a good home and even a best friend. At first we were afraid for Lucy's life since Labs are bred to swim out and retrieve ducks that have been shot, but she and Sinbad took to each other like a duck takes to water and became inseparable. Unfortunately Lucy is not housetrained, which means that Sinbad lives outside with her, which has involved fencing in the whole yard. Fortunately, I'm good with my hands, so I built the fence. But Sinbad barks at every delivery person, mailperson, and passing stranger. Rescuing the unwanted is a demanding activity.

Currently I am raising three kittens whose mother was hit by a car. The so-called neighbors who live two miles away left them in a box on our doorstep because my reputation for animal rescue has spread. They didn't know my brother saw them do it. He also found their dead cat in the road and figured out what had happened. After I gave the cat a decent burial it was either feed the kittens every two hours or deliver them to the gas chamber at the so-called Humane Society. My siblings are useless but I did get help from Millie. There's nothing more good-natured than a middle-aged part-golden retriever, even missing one eye (a story about her past life she has never been able to tell us). I figured that if wicked Sinbad could take to a duck, one-eyed Millie wouldn't mind a few kittens. So after every feeding, I curled them up together next to her warm stomach and they all went right to sleep, Millie included. I didn't get much sleep myself and my mom started clucking about it. At least if you're going to stay up all night nursing the entire animal kingdom, you need to eat some protein. My mom thinks a vegan diet is not enough to sustain a growing sixteen-year-old. Half the world is vegan, I say. Half the world has no choice, she says. You see the way we are. But I have to admit that it used to be worse.

What saved us—I mean, not saved by the Lord as my father would say but saved by life—was this Event. Before the Event my mother and I had gotten beyond arguing. We were not speaking at all. If you can't say something nice, don't say anything at all. That's not from the Bible, but it's my mother's creed. She was pregnant with Number Five and I had reminded her once too often about the ethics of overpopulation. So my dad was translating some heavy silence whenever the other kids weren't jabbering away. He kept talking about what the Lord giveth and I had to ask if the Lord hadn't ever heard of birth control. My mother left the table. Unfortunately my father had to leave for Bible camp after that and he took the rest of the family with him. Talk about silence. My mother had stayed home to get ready for the blessed event and I had just taken in an old wolfhound that somebody found chained up near an abandoned farmhouse. Well, it was mostly wolfhound, plus or minus a few breeds. My mother objected to this adoption. A wolfhound standing on its back legs sees eye to eye with a medium-sized human, which can be scary. Mostly they stand on four legs but it's good to remember their potential for equality. Surely my mother of all people could see that every creature born into the world deserves a chance. It's true that the dog had a major appetite, but being big shouldn't disqualify you from life.

Anyway, my mother was down in the basement opening up boxes of old baby clothes which she happened to have saved just in case the Lord blessed us again, and I was out back in the pen I had to build for the wolfhound so he wouldn't eat Sinbad's duck, when this enormous storm blew in. You read about storms like this in all the stories where the climax just happens to coincide with thunder and lightning but I swear it happened this way. The weather had been hot. I think that's why my mother was hiding in the basement all day. The air was tight around your body, like you could hardly breathe, like it was waiting for a blow-up, and my mother and I had the same feeling, like if either one of us spoke a word we'd both blow up. And then this heavy black cloud falls over my head and wind sizzles in my ears and I have the good sense to put Wolfgang in the empty garage and Sinbad and Lucy in the toolshed. Then I run for the kitchen door.

That's when I hear this strangled little voice calling me from the basement. I go down there and my mother is lying on the floor, sweat running down her face.

Mom, what's the matter, I ask like a dumbbell.

I think I'm having this baby, she says to me.

No, Mom, I yell at her like she can't hear me, it's not due till next month.

Don't argue with me now, we don't have time. I've had four babies and this one's coming. Go call the doctor and tell him to get out here fast.

Running up the stairs I almost get knocked over by a blast of thunder like dynamite and the whole kitchen lights up a puke shade of green. I pick up the phone and of course it's dead, just like in the movies. So I go back downstairs and Mom is gasping on the floor with her legs drawn up, breathing, breathing, breathing, and sweating.

Mom, there's no phone. I mean, the storm knocked it out.

You're going to have to help me then.

I can't, I can't, Mom, I don't know what to do.

You can. Go get that old mattress from the storage room and cover it with a clean sheet.

Suddenly she catches her breath again and can't

talk. I can't talk either because what's happening is way beyond words. I wrestle the mattress over to her and run upstairs for sheets. While I'm there I turn on the stove—thank God for gas stoves—and put water on to boil because that's what you read about. And I drop in a pair of scissors because when puppies get born the mother bites off the umbilical cord and I'm sure as heck not going to bite off this baby's umbilical cord. Plus I have to tie it off, right? That's what they show you in the medical books. I grab a spool of heavy thread from my mom's sewing basket and when I get back downstairs with the sheets and hot water and boiled scissors, my mother is grunting and yelling, and I start to cry while I sort of roll her over onto the mattress but then I stop because she's pushing and pushing and it feels like I'm pushing with her. Suddenly this little lump of wet head appears between her legs and out slips this sloppy little *fish-thing* right into my hands, which are covered with red blood and yellow cheesy stuff and tears dripping off my nose. Nobody told me that childbirth would be so *damp*. My mother's crying too now and pushing out the afterbirth and rain is pouring against the basement window. The whole world is wet and the baby's crying too because I clear out her mouth and turn her upside down and whack her just like I saw them do it on *Emergency One* and she burbles and breathes and lets out this tiny little wail. I cut some thread and tie the cord and cut the cord, just like they say you should, and then I wrap my baby sister in a sheet and put her on my mother's chest and the three of us just lie there holding each other, breathing.

Finally my mother tightens her arms around me and says in this real low voice right by my ear, I love you, Willa. And then, honest to God, there's this real low rumble of thunder like the storm is passing on and my mother puts my baby sister to her breast and starts nursing her.

Go see if the phone works yet, honey, she says to me, and I stumble up the stairs but the phone line is still dead and I'm not leaving my mother so I clean her and the baby up—finally I figure out what the hot water is for. Little Fish turns out to have arms and legs and fingers and toes, just the right number except extremely small. She also has hair as black as Sinbad's and slate blue eyes. Holding her hand in my hand, I lose my heart. My mother dozes off and on while I take care of them with blankets and broth and baby-holding. After about six hours the electricity comes back on and the doctor shows up and says what a hero I am and what a great job I did and he couldn't have done it better himself, and my mother smiles at me like rainbows.

My dad comes home and says thank the Lord it was me here with her and not him because he would have passed out first thing, which is true. My dad is good with words but he turns gray and green at the sight of blood. My brother and sisters gather around the baby whooping and hollering and scaring her to death till I hush them all up and chase them out of the room. And all this time my mom is just smiling at me like I did something right for the first time in my life.

Ever since then, my mom and I have done better. She doesn't go on and on about Sinbad wrecking the garden and Wolfgang eating us out of house and home and the kittens crawling underfoot with half-blind Millie tagging along after them, bringing them back to their box one by one to clean them up with her patient pink tongue until they get out again.

But I can't finish this story, "Lab." The first few lines are okay but then I get stuck. The whole point of this story is the kid figuring out what's right and wrong. I don't know why I have so much trouble with it, maybe because I just don't know enough about science and stuff like that. Like they say, you have to write about what you know. I guess if I did that I'd have to write about my mom and me, and about Sinbad and Lucy and Wolfgang and Millie and the kittens. It couldn't be that interesting.

restaurant

SAM DID NOT WANT TO GO on his parents' second honeymoon. He had not wanted to go on their first honeymoon, either, but evidently he was there. It was the unexpected prospect of having Sam that had persuaded his parents, who had been in love for years, to finally get married. For this they were eternally grateful to him. They were not only grateful, they were weird—his parents were too weird. Other kids went off to camp every summer. Sam went camping with his parents, or white-water rafting, or scuba diving, or something. It had been great when he was little. Now it was embarrassing. They did not seem to understand that a separation was in order. His mother and father still hugged him and they hugged each other. After fifteen years, his parents were still in love. Other parents came to school conferences separately or not at all. Sam's parents held hands. He could hardly bear it. Sometimes he made them walk a block ahead of him so nobody would guess they were his.

This summer was not only a celebration of the big fifteen—their anniversary and his birthday—it was also a Cultural Event. They had scrimped and saved for a trip to Italy. Very romantic. For them. Of course, he would be somewhat isolated since most Italian fifteen-year-olds spoke Italian and he did not. When he pointed this out, his parents laughed and said there were other ways of communicating— adolescents all over the world had discovered this. Very funny, very witty, his parents, and above all, enthusiastic, always enthusiastic. There would be great museums to tour, great works of art to see, great food to eat, great, great, great. Well, maybe the food would be okay. Sam liked pizza. So far, there had just been airplane food, a long ride with no place to put his legs, and jet lag in a hotel room with no television shows in English. However, tonight was the big night, their first Italian restaurant, guaranteed in all the guidebooks to provide ecstatic tastes for the most discriminating palate. Sam hoped they had something for the less discriminating palate.

His parents emerged from their room looking absurdly happy. His mother had on a blue dress which, he had to admit, made her look good. His father had looped a white silk scarf around his neck, which made him look ridiculous. They did not comment on his grubby old blue jeans but linked arms with him and bounced gaily toward the restaurant. How could you criticize your parents when they didn't criticize you? It was creepy, all this togetherness.

The restaurant was tiny. There were only a few tables, and the one in the middle was covered with dishes of food, from which you were supposed to choose an appetizer. It looked like there might be nothing for Sam to choose because everything had legs or tentacles that appeared to have been recently active in seawater. There were vegetables floating in olive oil and other tidbits that Sam felt also had left their natural habitat too far behind. And there was goat cheese that smelled like goat. His parents ordered a bottle of red wine. They were going to need it, from the look of the stuff on their plates. Sam got a coke and ordered what his mother swore, on her honor, was steak—grass fed. He did not like knowing what his steak had been fed, but his mother was so proud of translating the menu that he didn't have the heart to say anything. It was hard, though, to watch them swallow leggy appetizers while gazing deeply into each other's eyes. Only by looking around could he avoid the sight, and it was then that something caught his eye in a dark corner ...a dog carrier with its door open and a brown and white puppy curled up inside. No, not a puppy, a full-grown Jack Russell terrier, small but radiating confidence. It stirred, stood up, stretched with a needle-toothed yawn, circled three times for more comfortable positioning, and settled sleepily back onto its pillow. The two handsome young men dining with the dog carrier under their table were engrossed in each other.

Meanwhile, Sam's parents had finally stopped smiling and were looking at him with concern.

"Are you sure you won't taste some kind of appetizer?" asked his mother.

"What's that you're looking at?" asked his father

"The dog!" Sam whispered to his parents.

"Come on, Sam, there's no need to be insulting. These are delicacies even if you don't want to try them."

"No, no, in the corner, with those two guys ..."

Sam's mother and father turned around discreetly and then faced him again.

"It's just two men holding hands, Sam. Stop staring."

"No, it's not that! It's the dog. They brought their dog in here."

"The dog is very well behaved," said his mother. "I didn't even notice it. Anyway, it's a European custom, I've read about it."

"There's no sanitary law or anything?"

"Since when are you concerned about sanitation?" His mother smiled down at his jeans.

"I'm not! I just wondered . . ."

At that moment there was a commotion at the entrance. Framed in the doorway was a stunning woman, poured into a red dress and draped with gold chains, earrings, and bracelets. She carried in her arms a dog in miniature, a Maltese no more than five inches tall, weighing in at perhaps five pounds, its long white fur combed and tied out of its eyes with red ribbon.

"Oh, my gosh, it's like eating at the pound," said Sam.

"Shush," said his mother. "Keep your voice down. A lot of Italians speak English."

"But . . ."

"Sam," said his father.

"Okay, okay, I'm just saying . . ."

"When in Rome, do as the Romans do," said his mother.

"You wouldn't have let me bring Rover to Rome, Mom." Sam thought longingly of his old golden retriever, faithful to the last wag. Every sweep of his tail would have cleared the dishes off a table in this restaurant.

"Well, especially not after he died last year," said Mom.

The woman in red swept past their table cradling her Maltese. Behind her trotted a small sleek man and a girl dressed in black, as if she hoped no one would notice her. No one did, except Sam. As the three of them sat down, the woman fussed over her Maltese and the man fussed over the woman. The girl stared down at her napkin. Two waiters rushed over and focused a stream of Italian at the woman in red. They were joined shortly by a third man, perhaps the owner since he spoke the loudest. Evidently, the menu was no more to the woman's liking than it was to Sam's. She shook her head, firing word missiles at the waiters and her husband while cuddling the dog in her lap. Finally she waved her hand at the appetizers, whereupon her husband leaped up to fill two plates, both of which he set in front of her. Delicately, she began to sort through the legs and tentacles, dropping one bite neatly into the Maltese's mouth and then one into her own. The sleek man went back and took a modest helping for himself. The girl sat still. Only the woman and the Maltese seemed to be communicating.

"Don't stare, Sam. The one language everyone

understands is rudeness, and you are being rude. I don't want to say this again—please do not stare."

"Mom, how can I help it?"

"You've seen funnier things in Chicago."

"Only at the zoo."

"Spoken like a true American tourist."

"Okay, okay, I won't say anything then."

Sam slouched back in his chair and cultivated a sulk. His parents smirked at each other as if he were the world's greatest humorist and began to plan the next day's excursion. True to his word, Sam said nothing. He tried very hard not to look at the Maltese, but in the other direction were the two men and the Jack Russell terrier, which was snoring slightly. Where was Sam supposed to put his eyes? The dogs paid no attention to each other. The Jack Russell's eyes were closed, the Maltese's fastened on the next tentacle descending toward its mouth from a long pair of brightly painted fingernails. Sam's eyes swiveled between the two dogs like a periscope. That's how he caught the girl in black looking at him. She dropped her eyes immediately to the napkin. He did the same. Then they both raised their eyes, and some kind of beam shot through the air between them like a laser. She looked at the Jack Russell terrier, at the Maltese, and back at Sam. Then the corners of her mouth lifted in the tiniest smile

Sam had ever seen. Suddenly he could feel a shout of laughter fighting to rise through his body and surface in the space around him like a diver too long underwater. He tried to control it and snorted instead. Both of his parents drilled him with a look. The girl leaned over and spoke to her mother. First her mother shook her head, no, but the girl persisted, and after the Maltese had finished everything on its plate, the woman drew from her handbag a dainty red leather leash. She snapped it onto the Maltese's sparkling collar and handed it reluctantly to the girl, who slipped out of the restaurant like a shadow. The woman and her husband stared over each other's heads as if each were alone.

"Excuse me," said Sam to his parents. "I'm going to find the men's room."

"Okay, son, don't be long. Your steak will be ready soon."

Sam circled behind them, sidled past the bathroom, walked quickly through a chaotic kitchen, and found his way out the back door as the chef and busboy yelled Italian insults after him. Then he made his way around the block to the front entrance of the restaurant, where the girl in black stood waiting with the Maltese on a leash and the tiny smile on her face.

room 313

CLOTHES ARE HEAPED ON the bed, the chair, the desk, the floor. She has tried on everything in the closet. Nothing fits. Each item is uglier than the one lying under it, layers and layers of ugliness, like her own body. Someone in the universe has finally asked her out on a date and she will have to go naked. He will come to the door. He will stare. Mom will scream, Step-Dad will shout. Anne will shiver with cold—Headline: FASHION GOES STARK. She pulls on a pair of baggy jeans and a T-shirt. It is time to go to the hospital. If she does not get a good grade on this assignment, she will fail health sciences. Ms. Templeton is a terror. She has no right to require volunteer work, it's not fair. Volunteer work is supposed to be voluntary. Like reporting for the school paper, like all the other outside activities. What makes them outside and not inside? Whatever it is that outside activities are outside of, she will have to drop her outside activities if she fails health sciences—ACE REPORTER CUTS JOURNALISM CLUB.

She calls Snowy. What a name, Snowy. What a stupid little kid she was to give him that stupid name. Well, he was white, *is* white, is *still* called Snowy. He loves his name. He comes bounding across the room, seventy-five pounds of sweet-natured generosity, pure as the driven snow. All the clichés fit Snowy. There is no mean bone in his body. All his bones are thickly layered with lard. Labs tend to get chesty, says the kennel owner. Chesty. That could apply to more than Labs. She herself is chesty. And stomachy. They say dogs take on the characteristics of their masters. Mistresses.

Snowy sits down in front of her and waits for a command. When she doesn't give one, he hunkers closer in hopes of appearing yet more obedient. Snowy is very big on obedience. That is why he qualifies for the volunteer project. A lot of little kids are scared of dogs, especially sick little kids. Only a totally good-natured, obedient dog will cheer them up. If Snowy were mean and evil, Anne would be off the hook. He would tear up pillows and send patients screaming through the halls. DOG RUNS RAMPANT. FEATHERS FLY. How is it that they could only schedule her visit for the afternoon before her first date? How is it that this is only her first date? How is it that nothing fits her body? How is it that she is such a lump? How is it that her dog is such a lump? How is it that clichés swarm into the mind of an ace reporter like bees to honey?

Room 313 does not look promising. The child appears to be nothing more than a small lump under white covers. Because of the shaved head, Anne cannot tell whether it is a boy or a girl. The name Toby could go either way, and Toby is not telling. There are too many tubes for Toby to say much. Nose, mouth, and arms are all occupied by tubes. Toby's mother looks up at Anne with sad black circles under her eyes. She does not smile like the other parents did when they saw Snowy coming down the hallway. Snowy, who has heeled religiously beside Anne since they walked through the sliding front doors, who has wagged his tail at every child on the ward, who has affectionately snuffled those brave enough to pet him, does not wag his tail. He leaves Anne and pads slowly to the bedside, laying his muzzle on the covers near Toby's thin hand. For a while, Toby does not move. Then slowly the hand inches toward the soft muzzle. The fingers slide over Snowy's ears and nestle there, resting. Snowy's eyes close. Toby's eyes, which were half closed, close all the way. They look like a statue carved out of white marble. "Child with Dog."

The woman watches. "Toby always wanted a dog," she says finally. "But we're here so much." She gestures around the room as if it defines all time and space. Anne does not know what to say. How is Toby feeling today? Stupid question. What's wrong with Toby? Unkind question. Anne remembers what her immigrant grandmother used to say at funerals: *I'm sorry for your trouble.* Nana's troubles are over. She has passed beyond time and space. Anne wants to leave this room. It is late. This is taking much longer than she expected. This is supposed to be the happiest afternoon of her entire adolescent life. She begins to back out the door. "Snowy . . ."

Snowy opens his eyes and looks up at her patiently. He does not come. The fingers keep rubbing his ears.

"Toby really likes him," says the woman. "Maybe you could stay a little longer."

Anne takes a step forward, nods, and leans against the wall, waiting. She waits for ten minutes, for hours, forever. Nothing happens. How can nothing be so upsetting? At last she struggles against the silence that has been deadening her voice.

"We really have to go. I'm sorry." She has said it so many times in her head that she can't believe she has finally said it out loud. Too loud. The sound echoes off the walls. She crosses the room and snaps the leash onto Snowy's collar. She has not had to pull him away from anything since he graduated from obedience training.

As Snowy's head slides away, Toby's eyes flicker open and then close again.

"Thank you so much for coming," says the woman. "It means a lot."

"Maybe we can come again tomorrow," says Anne. "It's just that today I have this . . . I have to be somewhere."

The woman nods her head, and Anne escapes.

What is a date? This perfectly nice human being comes to the door and says hi and you say hi and you introduce him to your parents who just happen to be sitting around the living room. Your dog wags his tail politely and lolls his tongue out like the whole thing is too funny for words, which turns out to be true because after you say good-bye to the living room and head out the door, you don't know what to say next. There's plenty of time not to say anything, since you're walking to the movie because neither of you has a car or wants to hitch a ride with your parents. You look as nice as you can but too big. He looks as nice as he can but too small.

"So," you both say at once.

"What?" he asks.

"So what?" she asks. He laughs.

"Nothing," he says. They say nothing for a little longer. Two nothings in one day. It's a long way to the theater. Good thing they started early.

"So, what do you think of Journalism Club?" she asks. It is the only thing she knows they have in common.

"It's cool," he says. "I like digging around and finding things out."

"Do you?" she asks. "I like the writing part."

"That's the hard part, for me," he says.

"Not me, asking questions is the hard part for me. I think them but I can't say them. It's kind of scary, poking into people's lives."

"Yeah. The way I do it is sort of, I don't know, put this little space between me and them, so I'm not right in their faces, you know what I mean? And they're not right in mine."

"Like professional distance," she says. Their advisor's exact words, *professional distance*. They look at each other and smile.

"You got it," he says.

"Only in my head," she says. "I can't do it out loud." She thinks about the black circles under the woman's eyes and tries not to think about Toby tied to the bed with tubes of fluid running in and out.

"You have to practice," he says. Another favorite expression of their advisor's.

"Maybe tomorrow," she says. She wants to tell him about her health sciences project but this is a date. They are supposed to be having a good time. She should be asking him about himself, that's what all the magazines tell you, men find it flattering to talk about themselves. She could ask him what kind of music he likes.

"Are you doing a volunteer project for your health sciences class?" she asks. She cannot believe this question has come out of her mouth, about a subject she has just decided not to talk about.

"Yeah, I think we all have to. It's a requirement."

"So what are you doing?"

"Well, you know how Ms. Templeton is wild about diseases. I guess it's catching." He laughs, but Anne does not. "Anyway, I volunteered to collect money for the American Cancer Society. That's part of it, anyway. I have to collect a bunch of statistics and stuff, too, which I figured I could write up for the paper, maybe kick off a little fund-raising campaign in the school or something. How about you?"

"I . . ." The words clog up her throat. She tries
again. "I . . ." Why did she start this? There's a long
silence. "I take my dog to the children's hospital . . ."

"Hey, that's cool!" he says. She tries not to cry.

Anne and Snowy approach the front doors of the
hospital, which slide open silently. Today Anne
knows exactly where she is going, and Snowy trots
along beside her obligingly. They do not stop at any
of the other rooms but go straight toward 313. Today
Anne will stay all day, if Toby wants her to. It's
Sunday. Her first date is over, having improved con-
siderably after they got past the subject of health sciences projects. It is a new day now, a good day for
new beginnings. She has dressed carefully and looks
as nice as she can. Snowy looks as nice as he is. They
pause at the doorway and look in.

The room is empty. Sun slants across a bed
crisply made up with clean white sheets. The chair
sits by itself. A steel water pitcher twinkles on the
bedside table, with two glasses turned neatly upside
down beside it. The linoleum floor shines. It's the
wrong room. Anne takes a step back and looks over
the door. 313. She knows it was 313. She looks
inside again, steps back out, and looks up and down
the hall. Snowy waits. A nurse walks by and pauses.

"Hi," says the nurse. "You must be the new volunteer. The kids had a wonderful time with your dog yesterday. They're still talking about it."

Anne stares at her.

"Are you lost?" asks the nurse. "It's a real maze, this hospital."

Anne continues to stare at her.

"Are you looking for someone?"

"Toby," says Anne. "We came to see Toby yesterday. Did she go home?"

The nurse drops her eyes. "No, not exactly."

"So . . ."

"Toby died last night. She's been sick a long time." The nurse turns away a moment and then goes on. "It was so good for Toby to have a visit on her last day. Her mother said she loved your dog." The nurse leans over Snowy, who wags his tail obligingly.

Anne looks back into the room and says nothing.

"I know, it's hard," says the nurse, "but I hope you'll come back again." She pats Anne's back instead of Snowy's, and hurries down the hall into another room.

A kind of white space opens up in front of Anne. Wherever she turns there is nothing but air, and yet she can hardly breathe. How is it possible to be so chesty and so breathless? Her lungs feel full of earth instead of air. It's her head that's full of air, air heaped on air, white space swirling around and around. Maybe she will faint. She has never fainted before. Anne feels Snowy lean against her and feels herself leaning back against him, thankful suddenly for the anchor of both their solid bodies.

cargo

HISTORY HAS NOT BEEN kind to animals. You don't want to know the details, but man's (and woman's) best friend often fares the worst. If you built a museum documenting cruelty to dogs, its walls would stretch farther than bloodhounds can follow a fresh trail. And nobody would buy tickets. So I'm proposing we start a smaller museum, a little place to document kindness to dogs, something to pep us all up. It won't take much space, because human goodness seems to have some built-in limitations. We'll set it up in the countryside where dogs can enjoy it too. When they get tired of looking at the exhibits, they can pee on them. That's like signing the visitors' book—name and address liquefied.

I have an episode to contribute. It's a true story, reported in the newspapers, though only from the human point of view. I'm not much of a reader, myself, but I have a sharp ear and a good memory, and Walter has told his half of the story so many times that I know every word.

To begin with, we have to get back to that problem of humans' disregard for dogs, despite all the lip service paid to loyalty. The disregard is not always intentional. Humans just assume that nature is there for them to move around. A human in Texas wants an Alaskan husky, and bang, there it is, fur coat and all. Every degree of heat above freezing takes its toll—that's a one-hundred-degree-Fahrenheit toll, come summer.

The dog in this story has a slightly different problem. A Xoloitzcuintli is, to put it bluntly, hairless. Handsome, certainly, but vulnerable to conditions below zero degrees Fahrenheit, which are not uncommon on the windswept plains outside of Chicago. Illinois is a long way from Mexico, where this dog comes from, but humans love unusual dogs that make them feel unusual. Of course, Walter has always felt unusual, so when his parents offer him a dog in the interest of making him less unusual, he chooses a rare dog and naturally brings it to live where he lives.

When he is not attending high school, Walter is a shoe salesman, but he only sells soles with soul, Birkenstones, and he puts his whole heart into it. Walter has determined to make his life count in ways that puzzle his parents, who are stock investors. Walter earns his own money because he does not believe in the goals and values of the companies in which his parents invest. Although he suspects that some of his customers share those goals and values, he cannot convert the whole world at once. It is a matter of putting one foot in front of the other, in Birkenstones if possible. The first step has been to persuade the owner of the shoe store, an aging California hippie named Lillian who is sensitive to children and animals, to hire him after school and on weekends. His second step has been to persuade Lillian to let a dog accompany him to the store during those hours so that the dog will not be lonesome and children will be entertained while their parents buy Birkenstones, which often require tedious fittings and difficult decision-making. Choosing a pair of Birkenstones, Walter believes, is like making a friend. It takes time, and if you treat them right, they last for a lifetime. Walter does not have many friends, but he is patient and hopeful.

Enchanted with Walter's Xoloitzcuintli and impressed by its unusual characteristics, Lillian, too, has brought a Xoloitzcuintli up from Mexico. She practices pronouncing it correctly: *sho-lo-eats-queent-lee*. Now two Xoloitzcuintlis pad in and out of the Birkenstone fitting room, trembling throughout the winter when drafts from the arctic wind sweep through the door along with unwitting customers. Walter has knitted each dog a warm sweater, one green and one yellow to avoid gender stereotypes. He could have used some of his shoe-sales money to buy dog coats, but he is committed to living as simply as possible. Walter is also learning Spanish so that his dog does not feel culturally deprived. High school students like Walter are a rare breed.

Xoloitzcuintlis are silent animals, perhaps burdened by institutional memory. In the old days, some three thousand years ago, people speared them in the mouth with arrows and buried them with human remains to guide the deceased to heaven. No wonder they keep their mouths shut. However, I promised to spare you the details, and of course Walter would never dream of sacrificing his beloved Nina. Times change and, as I mentioned before, this is a heartwarming story.

It is spring vacation, and Walter is on his way to California. Lillian has offered him a week in her time-share beach house because she can't really spare the time away from Birkenstone Bliss at a time when people start thinking, even prematurely, about sandals. And Walter has become like a son to her, much more so than to his own parents, who have not quite gotten over the sight of dreadlocked Walter knitting a sweater for his hairless dog. Naturally, Walter's Xoloitzcuintli will accompany him to California. A week on the beach without Nina would not be good karma.

The plane revs up. Walter has explained to Nina that the ride may seem scary but the beach will make it all worthwhile. Though it is still icy in Illinois, southern California will be balmy. He has brought sunblock to protect Nina's skin. Walter is careful always to rub her skin with almond oil after her monthly bath and never cooking oil, which would cause sunburn if she were by any chance overexposed to brilliant sunlight. He has given her a little pill to keep her calm and has watched tenderly as the baggage handlers take her away in a portable crate. Now he settles into his seat at the back of the plane, buckles the safety belt, dons headphones, and thinks poetically about the cloud formations that billow around the plane as it gains altitude. He can stretch his legs—there is an empty seat beside him. The stewardess serves him a beverage of his choice.

Finally, Walter is so stirred by the beauty of the stratosphere that he pulls out his laptop, which his parents gave him in the hope that he would learn to make spreadsheets, and turns it on to record his thoughts. The screen saver is a photo of Nina, her body a color that Walter has always had trouble naming. It is the color of shade, the color of a shadow on the ground. But they are so far from the ground. Walter remembers that bit of Xoloitzcuintli history, how dogs were killed in order to guide their masters' souls to heaven, and feels uneasy.

Below him, in the plane's black cargo hold that has swallowed her, Nina feels cold. The pill has paralyzed her and the cold is digesting her. The cold first absorbs her nose and the tips of her large expressive ears, thin and membraned as a bat's. It takes hold of her toes and long thin tail. It climbs, now, up her four graceful legs a centimeter at a time, all way to the armpits where she sweats—when it's hot—like a human. Beyond her armpits the cold keeps creeping closer to her center. She would like to move, but the crate does not allow her much room and she is tired, so instead, she trembles. Nina trembles and shakes. Her teeth, fewer than other breeds' teeth because of a common genetic mutation, click like slivers of ice. Her body, usually hot to the touch with no fur for insulation, is clammy. She becomes stiff, like the red pottery dog statues of Colima that eventually were buried as replacements for real dogs. Nina knows only cold. She does not know that the baggage handler has mistakenly loaded her into the forward cargo hold instead of the heated rear hold.

Someone else knows——of course, Xolotl, an Aztec canine god who supervises the dead——but also Mike Johnson, a baggage supervisor who happens to be reviewing paperwork earlier than usual because he has a few minutes before his coffee break and doesn't have the energy to do anything else. Mike has been up most of the night with a cold, but he's awake enough to notice a duplicate animal crate record marked for the wrong cargo section. He has told the dispatcher, who has told the pilot, who has told the copilot, who has told a flight attendant. The dog may be dead already, they say, but if she's alive, she will certainly not make it to California. The only chance might be to divert the plane and land at Denver. That alone could take forty-five to sixty minutes. To do it, they would have to notify the owner, inform the passengers, and cope with protests. The pilot weighs the decision, a mountain of trouble on one hand, a molehill of dog on the other. He has split seconds to decide. He looks out at the clouds and sees, staring directly at him through the window, the little white terrier that used to sleep on his feet when he was ten years old. He turns and smiles at the copilot, who smiles at the attendant, who squares her shoulders and walks to the back of the plane and leans over Walter.

"Sir?" she asks quietly. Walter is listening to surfing music with his eyes closed and the screen saver glowing steadily. The attendant touches him lightly on the shoulder. Walter twitches and opens his eyes.

"Sir?" she says again, a little louder. "Your dog?"

"Yeah, she's a beauty, hunh?" says Walter, staring fondly at the screen.

"We have a problem with your dog."

As the attendant speaks, Walter's heart coagulates with grief and guilt. He leans his head against the chilly glass screen saver as the captain switches on the public-address system and explains why they are diverting to Denver. A long silence stretches its legs along the aisle while the passengers look at each other, then away. Some sigh. No one protests. Who wants to be the executioner? They have read about dogs fried alive during long delays on sizzling summer runways. This is a different story, but it is theirs whether they want to be in it or not. The only question is how it will end. There is nothing to do except wait and see if the dog has frozen to death.

The hour hangs over Walter like smoke on winter

air. He shivers, his eyes begin to glaze, and remorse drifts across him like snow. He feels his dog dying one frosty breath at a time—supposedly pain gives way to sleep. He squeezes a red airline blanket in his fists. When the plane finally bumps onto the ground and taxis to a gate, he can hardly stand up but wavers slowly, as if seasick, to the side of the attendant at the front of the plane. She whispers to him that a ground crew is standing by to pull Nina's crate from the cargo hold. She does not know why she is whispering except that the whole plane seems to be holding its breath.

Suddenly, the captain bursts out of the cockpit, thumbs up. "She's alive," he says. "Let's take a look." He guides Walter through the metallic doorway and down a ladder to the ground. Walter shoulders his way through the ground crew surrounding the crate and kneels down. Nina lies very still, but when he calls her name and opens the crate, her tail moves in a barely visible flicker of devotion. He folds her in the red blanket and cries. The captain looks at the supervisor.

"Can he take her on board?" asks the captain gently.

"It's against the rules," says the supervisor.

"This is an emergency situation," says the captain. "We're behind schedule and this dog needs personal attention."

The supervisor rubs his forehead and thinks about animal welfare and lawsuits. "Okay," he says. "Your responsibility."

"Yes," says the captain, "but no frequent flier miles for the dog." The supervisor stares at him.

"It's a joke," says the captain. He throws an arm around Walter, who staggers up the steps with Nina in his arms. The attendant brings up the rear with the crate. When they enter the plane, a collective cheer rocks the cabin. Eyes moisten up and down the aisle. Walter finds his seat and backs into it, holding Nina like a baby. Slowly she lifts her head and looks at him. He puts his face down to hers, and she delicately licks the end of his nose.

After the plane gains altitude again and the safety belt sign goes off, the flight attendant serves everyone free drinks. A little boy comes back with his mother and begs to pet Nina. Walter allows it, and another one comes back, and another. There are seven children on the flight, and when they have finished petting Nina, a few adults stray back as well. Nina is coming to life. She is always dignified, but she warms to the friendly strokes. As she thaws, her shivering subsides. She moves—she can move again—from Walter's arms into the seat beside him, piled with red blankets from surrounding passengers, and circles three times, pawing the blankets into a nest. Then she snuggles down with her head on Walter's knee and closes her eyes.

Walter rests his hand on her head and thinks about death, time, and space. He remembers the bits and pieces of history he has visited on the Xoloitzcuintli Web page—Aztec, Mexican, North American. It occurs to him that the last hour is now history, and he has partaken of it. Every present has a past. Walter digs his bare toes into Birkenstone leather. Perhaps he will study history.

the drive

"NOT NOW!"

"You promised, Clara. That was our deal. You get the car Friday night if you take Grandma for a drive Sunday afternoon."

"I've got a test tomorrow."

"You can study afterwards."

Clara finished her coffee and considered the privileges of being sixteen.

"Here are the keys, Clara. Drive carefully."

Clara stared out the window. The windowpane had frozen into a crystal map. She got up and grabbed her coat. Where was her stupid wallet? She was feeling for it in her pocket when Sadie lay down quietly in front of her, legs stretched straight, ready for a command. Wiley danced in circles, tail riotous, begging to go, preferably on a walk to sniff out rabbit poop. Wiley considered rabbit poop to be the popcorn of the canine universe.

"No, I don't think so. You two better stay here."

Both dogs drooped. They knew the fateful words.

"Why don't you take the dogs?" asked her mother. "Grandma would love to see them."

"But . . ." Clara paused at the door. "Oh come on, then."

They charged toward the car, and, as soon as Clara opened the back door, jumped onto the seat blanket with Border collie precision. Sadie curled up quietly on the side behind the steering wheel. You could drive Sadie for twenty-four hours and never know she was there. Wiley, whose mother was collie but whose father must have been a less rational breed, shifted constantly to stare through the front windows, which for some reason he preferred to the side view. Clara often glanced into the rearview mirror to find black ears framing her own head.

The nursing home was only a mile away. "Stay," she commanded as she locked the door and ran in to get Grandma. Always she felt stupid putting them on stay in a locked car. Where could they go? But *stay* structured their abandonment. They were placed, not forgotten. Once placed, a true Border collie knew exactly what to do and always did it. Be watchful. Don't move unless the occasion calls for it.

In the short distance between the parking lot and the nursing home, the sub-zero cold took her breath away. The dogs would feel it in the parked car, but they'd be all right for as long as it took to wheel Grandma out and load her into the front seat.

The room was dark when she walked in.

"Grandma?"

"Who's there? Is somebody there?"

"Hi, Grandma, it's Clara, how are you? We're going for a drive today, remember?"

"What day is it?"

"Sunday."

"What time is it?"

"It's two o'clock. You must have fallen asleep after lunch."

"You mean dinner."

"Well, whatever. It's dark because the shades are drawn. Come on, we have to hurry. I left the dogs in the car and it's freezing outside."

"Yes, I *am* cold, I've been thinking that. Could you get me another blanket?"

"It's not cold in *here,* Grandma—you just need to move around. I'll bring a blanket for you in the car.

Let's go." She shouldn't be impatient. She knew Grandma was always cold. Clara leaned over and braced herself for the precarious shift from bed to wheelchair. She could hear Grandma's bones creak in each knee and hip socket where the cartilage had worn away.

"At least you're all dressed and ready to go," said Clara. Grandma looked down at her clothes in surprise.

"So I am," she said amiably. "And I need my aspirin. Could you call the nurse?"

"Oh, Grandma, it will take forever to get her in here."

"But my knees . . ."

"Okay, we'll stop at a drugstore on the way and you can take your aspirin in the car. I can't leave those dogs out in the cold too long. I should have left the engine running to keep the car warm. I shouldn't have brought them in the first place."

"You brought the dogs?"

"Yes, yes! That's why we have to get moving. Lean forward so we can get this coat buttoned. Here, let me do it."

"But I have to go to the bathroom."

Clara could feel her back teeth clench. She made an effort to relax her jaw and shoulders.

"All right, Grandma. I'll help you." The labored

transfer from wheelchair to toilet seat and back again took longer than the deed itself. Finally, Clara was able to maneuver the chair through the door and down the hall.

"Stay here, now, Grandma, and I'll bring the car up."

"We're going out? Oh, Clara, how lovely! I haven't been out in so long. What day did you say it was?"

"Sunday."

Clara tied a scarf around Grandma's head before she ran out to the car. In the back seat, Sadie was wrapped into a doughnut shape with her tail over her nose. Wiley swiveled his ears like a weather vane and shivered forward at the sound of the unlocked door.

"Stay back. Sit! Good dog."

The car started with a reserved *chug-chug,* quiet and sturdy—not unlike Sadie, thought Clara, glancing toward the back seat. All she could see were Wiley's two black ears. Clara left the car idling to warm up as she ran back through the automatic doors, wheeled Grandma out, negotiated her into the front seat, and parked the wheelchair inside to await their return.

"Did you sign her out?" asked the nurse.

"No, I forgot." Clara reached over the nurses'

counter and scribbled Grandma's name, her own name, the date, the time, and the time of expected return. Under *destination,* she paused.

"We're just going for a drive today."

"That's fine, but be careful. Your grandmother is so fragile."

"I know," said Clara. She unlocked her jaw again and hurried back out to the car, where Grandma dozed, Sadie waited, and Wiley wagged his tail. Lord, it was cold.

"It's so beautiful out," said Grandma suddenly.

Clara swept her eyes across the cornfields, brittle under wind-etched snow.

"And the car is so cozy. Your grandfather loved this car. He used to drive me to the drugstore just to show it off. You're lucky, Clara. Not everybody inherits a Mercedes."

"It's forty years old, Grandma. We can hardly afford to keep it going anymore." But she loved the car. Solid as a tank, it had sheltered her across the countryside for as long as she could remember, first in Grandma's arms up front and later in the back seat, safe within the moving walls of the family's weekly adventures. This car had rocked her to sleep and wakened her to the world. It was the sole inheritance from her grandfather's long-gone fortune. They would never part with it.

"I need my aspirin," said Grandma suddenly.

"Oh, Grandma, are you sure? We're just going to be out for about an hour. I wanted to swing through Salt Fork State Park to see the snow on the fir trees."

"But my knees hurt so, my knees . . ."

"All right, we'll stop at the mall. That's closest."

Clara looked to the right, where the highway stretched into stunning isolation, and then turned left past the fast-food strip to a mammoth covered mall. The parking lot was jammed. She finally found a spot, right beside a pole with a red ribbon dangling around it like a holiday afterthought. She'd have to leave the car running this time, but it was only for a minute.

"Stay," she commanded the dogs.

"Yes, I will," said Grandma. "I'm really not up to walking today, if you don't mind."

Or any other day, thought Clara, whether I mind or not—but don't be cross with her. She's old and helpless. I'm young and healthy. She was good to me, I will be good to her. Where's the darn drugstore in this maze? Feeling the car idling in her bloodstream, Clara threw herself into high gear toward the aspirin.

He couldn't believe his luck. A vintage Mercedes in mint condition, purring like a kitten with the keys inside and nothing but an old lady nodding off in the front seat. Like one of those mirages people see in the sand dunes that turn out to be real water. He looked around at the desert of cold, lonely cars and eased open the door. She didn't even wake up. Shoot, there was a dog. But it looked friendly. Yeah, it was wagging its tail. Big ears, small brain, no problem. Could you believe somebody would leave this baby running? It was an invitation: please take me. He could dump the passengers later on a country road. The cold would take care of them both. He eased into gear. The car in the space ahead of him was pulling away. Unbelievable—he didn't even have to back up. He could swing around the next couple of parking aisles and head for the highway. Piece of cake.

He was into the third aisle when he felt something wet close around his neck, first gently, then with the pressure of teeth. It wasn't the dog, he could see the dog in the rearview mirror, panting with a big grin on its face. What? What was it? A haunted car? He couldn't even move his head. The Hook? The teeth tightened. Pain and terror bit deep into him and he hit the brake and reached for the door handle. With a final squeeze, the teeth released him into the snapping cold. He slammed the door to keep whatever it was in the car and ran headlong toward the mall, where normal people scurried in and out of the automatic doors.

"Are you back already, dear? Did you get my aspirin?" asked Grandma.

No one answered.

Clara jiggled in line like a child desperate to pee. Who could believe there'd be post-Christmas returns and exchanges at a drugstore? She almost abandoned the aspirin and bottle of water on the counter when the woman ahead of her paid for a huge purchase with a credit card, and the number had to be punched in because the strip was worn. Finally, it was Clara's turn. She slapped a five-dollar bill down on the counter, grabbed the change, and made for the door.

"Don't you want your receipt?" called the cashier.

"Keep it!" shouted Clara, and charged through shoppers combing the January sales for bargain prices.

Once outside, she made for the parking aisle where she had left the car. Or thought she had left the car. Surely . . . No, she remembered the pole with the red ribbon around it. So where was the car? Was her mind going, like Grandma's? Was it contagious? She raced down one parking aisle and up the next, panting now and clutching the aspirin like a talisman. There. There. No, not a Mercedes, an imitation. God, what if Grandma had . . . no, she couldn't . . . she didn't even drive in her younger years. There. Oh, thank God. Safe and sound and still idling away, warm under a blanket of frozen air.

She eased open the door and stuck her head in.

"Everything okay?" she called to Grandma. Wiley wriggled forward, tail a-spin. Straining to peer into the back, Clara could just make out Sadie, black and white fur against black leather and white blanket, barely visible in her camouflage but for one gleaming eye. Good dog, hadn't moved a muscle. But she wouldn't bring them next time. This whole drive had gotten too complicated. How could she have forgotten where she'd parked? It was stress, that's what it was: the cold, the dogs, the mother, the grandmother, the test tomorrow, and now a childproof medicine cap! How could any normal person cope? Especially with freezing fingers. Finally, through a mysterious accident of pushing, pulling, and turning that she could never repeat, Clara got the cap open.

"Here's your aspirin, Grandma, and some water to take it with." She handed her grandmother two aspirin and the plastic bottle of Purely Yours. Wiley surged forward and licked her ear.

"Stay back!" she said crossly. "Sit! This is not for you."

"Be good to the dogs," said Grandma, "and they will be good to you."

Clara made a face at Wiley in the rearview mirror. Then she shifted gears and eased down the aisle toward the Exit sign. Ahead of them, the black highway stretched toward a white sun whose eye gleamed on the snowy fields.

a grave situation

"LISTEN TO THIS, SOREL."
Colin snapped the *News-Gazette* in an exact imitation
of their uncle. "'Stetson is a neutered four-year-old
healer mix. He is calm, intelligent, and good-natured
and is available for adoption at the Champaign
County Humane Society, 1911 East Main Street,
Urbana.' Here's the picture—see, he's got one blue
eye and one brown eye but they're both sad. Maybe
if I left this on the kitchen table, somebody would
get the hint."

"Give it up, Colin. They've got enough on their
hands with *us*." She meant *him*. She meant doctor
appointments, therapy sessions, surgery, hospital

visits, and medical equipment. She jumped up from the couch and charged toward the door.

"No, wait, here's something else," said Colin. Sorel stopped and turned halfway around.

"LOYAL TO THE GRAVE," he read slowly and dramatically. "Hey, Sorel, wait up. Where are you going? That was just the headline. Here's the good part. 'A grieving sheepdog left the home of his new owners in Cheshire, England, and set out on a sad journey last Christmas Eve to find the grave of his deceased master, a place he had never been. The Border collie Spot traveled four miles from his new home, dodging traffic on main highways, until he eventually found the cemetery where the farmer who had been his owner was buried. A local policeman found Spot, lying directly on the grave of his master in the yard of Saint James Church. The dog was then taken to the home of the trainer where he was born. The trainer plans to enter Spot in local sheepdog trials.'" Colin looked up at Sorel. "It's January twenty-fourth now. I wonder how he's doing."

"Why don't you write him and find out?" asked Sorel dryly.

"Maybe I will," said Colin.

"Just how are you going to get Spot's address?"

"Off the Internet. I'll e-mail the newspaper and track it down. See here, it says 'Syndicate E-mail: mail@worldupdate.com.'"

"You're nuts, Colin."

"You're jealous."

"Why in the world would I be jealous of a nutsy little brother?"

"Because you didn't think of it."

Sorel rolled her eyes and left the room.

Colin wheeled over and turned on the computer. While it booted up, he took a scissors, cut out the two pieces he had read aloud, and put them in his dog folder on top of a clipping from last week with a photo captioned: "A greyhound, Shadow, pictured at yesterday's protest by animal rights groups outside the capitol." The dog was a soft cloud-gray and looked as if it could float through the air. Instead, it sat on the concrete with a sign around its neck saying SAVE US PLEASE! Of course, those were human words. The dog just talked with its eyes. How could a greyhound know it would get destroyed if it didn't win at the racetrack? After Colin closed the folder, he turned over the cut-up newspaper he was about to throw away and saw a column boxed by a black line. "Your Horoscope," it said. "Your Birthday Thursday: Exciting developments concerning involvements with large organizations could be in the offing for you this year. Just be careful you don't bite off more than you can chew."

"Hey, Sorel, listen to this!" he yelled, but she did not answer, as she often didn't, so he opened his

E-mail. There were lots of new messages from people in places he would go someday—New York, Montana, Louisiana, Alaska. Just thinking about those places made him want to hop on a plane. But not right now. There was the dog-lovers' chat room to visit and the animal rights listserv to catch up on and the inquiries to make about Spot and maybe Stetson, just to see if he had been adopted yet with his one brown eye and one blue eye equally yearning for a home. There was so much to do before his teacher got here. And she'd want to check the lessons that he hadn't finished from yesterday. Colin began tapping at the keyboard.

Date: Mon., 24 Ja 2000 7:30:44
From: colin malone
(comalone@globalconnect.com)
To: champaign county Humane society
(cchs@champaign.org)
subject: stetson
Hi, I saw your picture of stetson in the paper today and wondered if he is a large dog or a small dog. Also, is he quiet or does he jump around a lot? A friend of mine wants to know. Thanks.

Date: Mon., 24 Ja 2000 7:33:27
From: colin malone
(comalone@globalconnect.com)

TO: mail@worldupdate.com
subject: spot

Hi, I saw your story about the sheepdog spot who tracked down the grave of his
old master and then got taken back to where
he was born. could you please find out how
he's doing and let me know? or send me the
address where they took him and i'll
write. thank you.

http://www.soga.org
Welcome to the Web page directory of
SOGA Save Our Greyhounds Association!!! Take
a tour of the SOGA Web site! Visit Silver and Jet
at home with their new foster families! Check
out SOGA's new projects for greyhound rescue!
Want to join up? Email us at dogdays@soga.org!
One of our volunteers will contact you!

Date: Mon, 24 Ja 2000 7:50:15
From: colin malone
(comalone@globalconnect.com)
TO: save our greyhounds Association
(dogdays@soga.org)
subject: shadow

Hi, I saw the picture of shadow in the
newspaper article that told about the
animal rights protest outside the capitol
last weekend and wanted to make sure somebody saved him. He's so thin I guess that's

why he's called shadow. i bet he runs fast even if he lost some races. would you please let me know what happens to him? thanks.

DATE: MON, 24 Ja 2000 8:00:09
FROM: colin malone
(comalone@globalconnect.com)
TO: sorel malone
(somalone@globalconnect.com)
subject: mad
Hi sorel, are you mad at me? you always go to school without saying good-bye.

DATE: TU, 25 Ja 2000 11:25:00
FROM: leo starsky
(lstarsky@downtime.com)
TO: colin malone
(comalone@globalconnect.com)
subject: shadow
Hello, colin, thanks for asking about shadow. we think that he has found a good home, but there are thousands more like him. are you interested in adopting a greyhound? i'm a volunteer in soga and the proud owner of two greyhounds that would have died if somebody hadn't cared enough to take them in. How did you get interested in greyhounds?

Date: Tu, 25 Ja 2000 12:25:33
From: Colin Malone
(comalone@globalconnect.com)
To: Leo Starsky
(Lstarsky@downtime.com)
Subject: shadow

Hi, Leo, I like all dogs, to tell you the truth, but it seems like greyhounds are just about the most graceful things in the world. I love the way they run, and I don't mean racing, but just kind of bounding along like an antelope or something. I saw this program on TV about greyhounds and it made me want to be one. I don't think I can adopt a greyhound though. Last summer my parents got killed in a car crash and my aunt and uncle take care of me, which is not easy because I can't walk since the accident. My sister says they are doing their best to deal with the worst. My sister could help take care of a dog but she won't. She's always in a snit. Anyway, I'm glad shadow's found a place to be. I could never keep up with a greyhound. My horoscope says don't bite off more than you can chew.

Date: Tu, 25 Ja 2000 16:39:20
From: sorel Malone
(somalone@globalconnect.com)

TO: colin malone
(comalone@globalconnect.com)
subject: mad
Don't be a goof. I'm not mad at you.
You're just used to everybody paying
attention to you all the time.

Date: Tu, 26 Ja 2000 18:25:00
From: Leo starsky
(Lstarsky@downtime.com)
TO: colin malone
(comalone@globalconnect.com)
subject: shadow
Gee, colin, that's a pretty tough situation. You really made me do some hard
thinking. I mean, here I am, worried about
these greyhounds all the time when there
are so many people to worry about.

Date: Tu, 26 Ja 2000 19:17:35
From: colin malone
(comalone@globalconnect.com)
TO: Leo starsky
(Lstarsky@downtime.com)
subject: shadow
Don't worry, I'm really okay except for
my legs. It's my sister who's the problem.
see, she was at summer camp and we were
driving up to visit on Family Day when this
gigantic tractor-trailer ran into our car

and she has been really mean ever since then. she was nice before. i don't know what happened to her—i mean, it's not like she got hurt or anything. our aunt and uncle are really nice, even though they never had any kids of their own. i don't think me and my sister are much of a door prize.

> DATE: TU, 26 ja 2000 20:13:05
> FROM: Leo starsky
> (Lstarsky@downtime.com)
> TO: colin malone
> (comalone@globalconnect.com)
> subject: shadow

Hey, colin, being an only child myself, i don't know much about sisters but i can take a wild guess. she might be feeling kind of guilty about why this stuff happened. Here she is, tucked away safe and sound at camp, and the whole family gets zapped because they're coming to see her. plus, this might sound weird, but it seems like she got left out of this huge thing that happened. it's like dogs. They get kind of spooked when a pack mate gets hurt or comes back from the vet, like with surgery or something. You know, the ones at home skulk around and act weird. i mean, i'm not saying your sister's a dog or anything,

but she might have got hurt inside. It's
worth thinking about. I've got to sign off
now and pick up my girlfriend. Keep in
touch.

> Date: Tu, 25 Ja 2000 21:14:11
> From: Colin Malone
> [comalone@globalconnect.com]
> To: Sorel Malone
> [somalone@globalconnect.com]
> Subject: Mad

Good night, Sorel. No matter how mean
you act you are still my favorite sister,
even if you are also my only sister. Ha ha.
I hope you feel better tomorrow.

> Date: Tu, 25 Ja 2000 21:19:33
> From: Sorel Malone
> [somalone@globalconnect.com]
> To: Colin Malone
> [comalone@globalconnect.com]
> Subject: Mad

What's wrong with you, twerp? I feel
fine. It's you that's sick all the time.
But good night anyway.

> Date: Wed, 26 Ja 2000 9:55:23
> From: mail@worldupdate.com
> To: Colin Malone
> [comalone@globalconnect.com]

subject: spot

we're sorry to say that we have no further information on spot. His new owner has not answered our calls. The graveyard attendant does say that the dog has not been seen near his master's grave since he was taken away at christmastime. Thank you for keeping up-to-date with world update.

DATE: wed, 26 ja 2000 16:57:11
FROM: champaign county Humane society
(cchs@champaign.org)
TO: colin Malone
(comalone@globalconnect.com)
subject: stetson

You and your friend will be happy to learn that stetson has indeed found a home. He's such a calm and friendly dog that it didn't take long. In fact, his new owner is picking him up this afternoon. Many others are not so fortunate, however. We have a saying here at cchs, Get a life, get a pet. There's one waiting for you. Visit cchs soon!

DATE: Th, 27 ja 2000 6:00:00
FROM: sorel Malone
(somalone@globalconnect.com)
TO: colin Malone
(comalone@globalconnect.com)

subject: stetson

If you ever wake up this morning lazy
brother you are allowed to come into my
room. I have a surprise for you if you can
guess this riddle. what has one blue eye
and one brown eye, and neither eye is sad?
Happy birthday.

fiona and tim

FIONA WAS SLOW AND SILENT, but all children have their own ways. In an Irish family of eight girls, slow and silent are lost in the general din. Her mother paid very little attention to her. It seemed the best way to cope, overall, and Fiona did not demand attention. From the beginning the girl lived in a world of her own and looked different as well. In contrast to her seven redheaded, rosy-cheeked sisters, Fiona had mousy brown hair and colorless skin. Her sisters secretly believed that she was a changeling whom the fairies had swapped for their real baby sister, stolen away at birth. As for Fiona's father, he paid her no attention at all. The man was overwhelmed by a steady stream of daughters who subjected him to harassment at home and teasing from the lads when he retreated for a pint at the pub. What was wrong with Fiona, as far as he was concerned, was being female. Beyond that he didn't know—since in those days there was no money for doctors or tests—and perhaps he couldn't care. There was just the farm and the endless work on it. A slow child who listened no better than she talked, which was never, seemed useless compared to the others, who could at least help their mother. Fiona would never have found her work on the farm had it not been for Tim.

Tim was quiet, too, but not slow—one of a hearty litter born the same time as Fiona. The puppies were all black furred with white legs, white ruffs, white tail tips. But only Tim had large brown eyes ringed with tan—luminous eyes. When his brothers and sisters went to other homes, Tim stayed, and he and Fiona played like twins. When she first crawled across the cottage floor toward the open doorway, he waited patiently outside where a dog belonged and nuzzled her as she came within reach. When she continued into the yard on all fours, he followed her toes. When later she rose to walk, pulling on the fur of his back, he stood steady, though only a yearling. When she learned to run, he ran ahead of her. One chased the other. The other chased the one. They rolled in the grass and mud. They fell asleep piled in a heap of matted fur and sticky hair and bones as light as bird wings. Awake, Fiona watched Tim without a word—she seemed to have no words—and turned her head to look where he turned his head to look. And Tim watched Fiona, herding her around the yard or toward the door when her mother called. Tim paid attention.

Fiona began to wander, for where Tim went she went as well, and Tim went with the sheep.

"Born to it," said Fiona's father, and he began to train Tim for the work of rounding up the flock, sending him to circle them with a wave of his arm, dropping him to the ground with a drop of his hand. Fiona watched and imitated his signals and followed when she could, but their land stretched up a stony mountain and their sheep scattered along cliffs that dropped into the sea.

"Go home, Fiona," shouted her father, and when he waved her away, she followed the direction of his hand, went back to the house, and waited for Tim to come home. If her father drove the sheep along the dirt road to another part of the mountain for fresh grazing, Fiona followed until they cut up over the steep rocks. Then she obeyed her father's fierce hand waving her away, and she walked back alone, watch-ing whatever came toward her, sometimes a furtive fox or a donkey-drawn cart, rarely a car. Cars were common in the city but still a new thing to the villagers, who stopped and stared as the dust rose along the road, encircled them, and settled down again— or else the mud sailed in wet sheets that made them jump onto the verge. Drivers tooted their horns at the backward farmers covered with dust or mud. Nobody in the village had a car yet, although they all wanted one. For Fiona's family wanting a car was like wanting the moon. Yet she saw cars sometimes and watched them carefully, the way she watched everything, waving her hand if anyone in the car waved at her, copying their signals exactly.

Tim did not like cars. Their smell choked him. They were loud, threatening, and predatory— strangers invading his territory. It was his obligation as a dog of honor to chase them away. When he heard a car coming he crouched by the road eyeing it intensely until it came close enough to rush. Then he ran, first alongside and then behind, barking furiously despite the fact that he rarely barked, until it was a safe distance away. If a car came along the road while he was herding the sheep, he confronted it with a snarl and then raced around behind the flock trying to herd them up the mountain out of harm's way, taking one last dash after the car as it rolled by. If Fiona saw a car coming, she tried to hold him back, but he struggled against her and was stronger.

The day they found out what was wrong with Fiona, it was too foggy to see a car coming. The fog had sneaked in off the sea, muffled each creature, and set every object in a world of its own. The purple foxglove, the orange crocosima, the flaming berries clustered on the rowan trees were all wrapped in gray. You could see your hand at the end of your arm and that was all. But sheep must eat whatever the weather. Fiona's father had planned to herd them farther along the mountain that day and only a gale could persuade him otherwise. He was leading the sheep down the road, with Tim bringing up the rear and Fiona trotting beside him.

The car swept around a sharp curve, the driver blind to all but the gray blanket wrapped around his windows. Tim heard it suddenly behind them. There was no time to confront the car, to snarl and bark and scare it away. He simply hurled himself against Fiona's body. She toppled into the ditch beside the road while the car caught Tim full on the flank and tossed him in the air as if it were a mad bull. Fiona lay in the ditch shaking and Tim lay still where he landed. Too late, the driver slammed on his brakes and honked the horn. The sheep scattered. Fiona's father turned back, peering into the fog, almost running into the driver as he swung open the car door.

"I didn't see her," shouted the man. "Could she not hear me coming?" Then he choked out an apology that was, in turn, strangled by the fog.

Fiona's father leaped into the ditch and picked her up in his arms. "Are you hurt, girl?" he breathed. "You're all right now, aren't you?" There was no blood that he could see, no broken bones that he could feel.

"I don't think she's hurt," said the driver. "She fell into the ditch. The dog knocked her out of the way."

"Tim?" called Fiona's father. Tim did not appear. They found him not too far away, and with him the blood and broken bones.

Fiona's father felt that it would be a kindness to kill the dog then and there, but Fiona, as if she sensed his plan, hovered over Tim, shielding him, in turn, with her own body. And so her father, seeing her demand something for the first time in her life, even soundlessly, laid Tim on his coat and let the driver take them home. He would send a neighbor to check on the sheep, and he would do what he could to staunch the blood and set the bones.

Tim lay quiet on a blanket by the fire. For two weeks they did not know whether he would live or die, and for two weeks Fiona slept beside him, ate beside him, stroked his ears, lifted his head a bit to squeeze wet rags into his mouth. And for the first time her father paid attention. He watched her take care of the dog with a skill she had never shown in anything else. He puzzled over her silence. And he heard again and again in his mind the stranger's question: "Could she not hear me coming?" At last one day he stood behind her and clapped his huge red hands together just behind her head. Again, again, again. She did not move but sat silently gazing down at the dog, which had lifted its head without Fiona's help for the first time at the sound of thunderous clapping. And then Fiona's father knew that Fiona was deaf, and perhaps dumb, but not dim or daft or half-witted or any of the other things they had assumed. And he knew that she could work a dog. And he knew that even if he did not have a son, he had someone who could help him work the sheep. He put his hand gently on her head and she turned around, surprised at the touch.

the nose

IT HAD A LIFE OF ITS OWN, and James followed it. He was not a hero. He was too stupid to be a hero unless heroes were stupid, which was a possibility. But he had a nose and he could not resist its call—to food, to adventure, to trouble, often in that order. It was an ordinary looking, moist nose, not outsized. You noticed it mostly because the rest of James was hidden under a mass of wiry gray fur. Nose and tail were all that counted when you saw James, and it was his tail that seemed most expressive, curved upward in a cheerful half-circle, a sort of permanent smile that reassured you everything was all right no matter what his nose had gotten him into.

James's family was also quite ordinary looking. There were four children, a mother, a father, and a grandfather who talked volubly to his wife of fifty years, the last ten of which she had been dead. Since they never fought anymore, it was an amiable arrangement. Life seemed normal for everyone in the family. Like James's tail, the children were probably what stood out most, two older boys and twin girls. Also like James's tail, they were generally cheerful, sporting smiles that reassured you everything was all right no matter what they had gotten into.

James's nose often got him into garbage. The possibility of scraps, however wilted and aged, enchanted him. The more mold and mildew, the merrier. Fuzzy, greenish pieces of unidentified meat only whet his appetite for whatever lay piled beneath them, in whatever rancid heap he might have sniffed out. Though not picky, James was persistent. He never stopped once his nose was in the air. It was a principle with the family to head a different way, preferably in the opposite direction, because following James would often lead to something disgusting. There was an exception to this rule, however, and her name was Laurel. Laurel was the younger twin, born five minutes after her sister, and smaller from the first breath. The doctors assured Laurel's parents that she was just as normal as the rest of the family, so they stopped worrying about her birdlike stature and got on with life.

Though small, Laurel was fearless in the face of garbage. She could never keep up with her twin but seemed perfectly attuned to James, who sat devotedly at her feet as various bits of food dropped first from her high chair and later from her fingers. James did not mind baby drool and Laurel did not mind dog slobber. As they both progressed in age, so did their attachment, based on a mutual curiosity about the possibilities of trash. In the early stages, Laurel was a toddler who overturned wastebaskets, examined each item, and taste-tested it before going on to the next. James was never far behind. Later on Laurel would hunker down over swampy puddles to look at the insect life developing there while James lapped it up, larvae and all. Laurel sketched the skeleton of a dead mouse while James decided whether to eat it. When Laurel graduated to her first microscope, James sometimes grew impatient, but their field trips still led them in a common direction. Laurel was liable to dissect the kind of thing James's nose detected.

Where James was persistent, Laurel was thor-ough. In fact, the whole family was nothing if not routine in their habits. Every day for years the mother and father went to work, the two boys practiced basketball, the older twin wrote poetry, Grandfather talked to his deceased wife Adelaide, and Laurel peered through her thick glasses to follow James's nose. Then it happened, as it sometimes does, that life got out of hand. The father lost his job and shortly afterwards, his happy disposition. The mother took a second job and was rarely home when she was needed. The two boys tested into a private school whose expensive tuition was not quite covered by their athletic scholarship. The older twin realized that her writing career could go no further without a computer. Laurel needed corrective eye surgery. Grandfather's faith in Adelaide began to falter, along with his mind. Only James held steady, his nose unwavering in its devotion to garbage. Everything else disintegrated.

Sensing the worst, Grandfather decided to move away with Adelaide. Maybe it was his defective hearing aid that made her voice so faint, but he didn't think so. She needed to get away from the tension that had suddenly enveloped the entire household. Grandfather packed carefully. His dutiful engineering career at Consolidated Electric had taught him to hoard things. Long after retirement, he still wound leftover string or wire into coils and stashed them away, often in places where he could never find them again. It was time to throw out a lot of the old stuff that had been lying around his room forever. He laid a suitcase out on his bed and snapped open a large garbage bag beside it on the floor. By the time the family came home from work, school, and job-hunting, the room was empty and Grandfather was gone. James scratched anxiously at the back door, wanting to go out.

There was an uproar. The neighbors were alerted. The police were called. Handmade signs were posted. Everyone in the family fanned out to look for Grandfather. They had hoped briefly that James might help track him down, but it was useless. James went only as far as the garbage cans waiting for pick-up in the back alley and then stopped. The mother cried and said she should have been more watchful. The father argued with the police and suggested they hire a private detective. The two boys vowed to scour the city. The older twin retreated to write sad poems about losing a loved one. Only Laurel kept an eye on James, who seemed unusually determined to get at the garbage cans. Generally he went farther afield, having been yelled at for knocking them over so many times. Today, he circled them repeatedly, gently shouldered one over, and ripped the top bag open with his teeth. Laurel did not interfere. She was curious, and she didn't mind cleaning up after him. At some level she trusted James to find treasure in the trash as he had done so often before, even though not everyone recognized true value when they saw it.

James's attention immediately fastened on an ancient doughnut encrusted with pipe tobacco. Laurel leaned closer. The only person in the house who smoked a pipe was Grandfather. Undeterred by the tobacco, James chewed thoughtfully on the doughnut, swallowed it down, and pawed deeper into the plastic bag. Out tumbled a quantity of junk—outdated coupons, used tissues, photographs faded beyond recognition, and magazines, interspersed with fossilized apple cores, stale cookies, candy wrappers stuck together by their melted contents—enough tidbits to keep a nose interested. Several odd bugs were already competing for James's snack and Laurel's attention. One of them clearly belonged in her bug collection, and she sorted through the rubbish looking for a container to capture it. Close to the bottom was an old cloth bag containing a handful of folded yellowing papers. She pulled them out to free the bag and noticed the words, in large black print, CONSOLIDATED ELECTRIC CERTIFICATE OF STOCK. Laurel was not stupid. She emptied a box of antique cough drops into James's mouth, captured the bug in the box, and went to show her father the bag of papers.

If this were a realistic story, the Consolidated Electric stock certificates would turn out to be worthless. Fortunately, it is true rather than realistic. Fairy tale endings can happen to quite ordinary people. It did not take long to clean up after James. It did not take long to discover the family was financially stabilized. Nor did it take long to find Grandfather. He had stopped by the drugstore to buy more cough drops when the pharmacist noticed him talking to Adelaide and called the police. As the family settled back into happier times, Grandfather settled back into his room with Adelaide, who seemed to appreciate the way he had cleaned things up. The mother of the family quit both her jobs and enjoyed a flexible schedule helping the father negotiate their investments. The two boys became basketball stars at their private school. The older twin got a laptop. After successful eye surgery, Laurel entered a program for gifted young scientists. And James became a hero.

nameless creek

MY DAD AND I DON'T TALK
much. Mama did most of the talking, so it's real quiet
now. Most of the time you can hear the wind blow-
ing across the fields. On a still day you can almost
hear the sun shining. The prairie's like that, either
blown or baked. In winter, it blows. We'd gotten such
low prices for our corn and soy crops that Dad was
taking on odd jobs hauling freight. His rig was old,
but it still worked if you treated it right—no sudden
stops and starts, no pushing for high-speed deliver-
ies, which meant you started early and kept a steady
pace. I got out of school for the holidays the day Dad
got this big job. He didn't want to leave me alone, so

we decided to make a night of it in the city, dinner out, movie, motel, the full monty. *The Full Monty* is my favorite movie. There's a boy in it kind of like me except my mama took off and left us. Dad and I saw *The Full Monty* in the city on one of our fun trips hauling stuff in the truck. Since then we've rented it so many times that either one of us could go make popcorn in the kitchen and bring it back and know what would be happening the whole time. We still cheered when those guys threw off all their clothes at the end.

I was excited about the trip, being in the truck with Dad, eating out. Dad's cooking was okay but kind of limited. We pretty much ate the same thing all the time: macaroni and cheese, hot dogs, potatoes, some peas here and there, canned peaches. I made peanut butter sandwiches to take with us for lunch, because once you got on the road with Dad's rig, you didn't stop. That morning he only drank one cup of coffee. You can't pee out the window of a moving vehicle.

We were going down the road listening to an old George Jones song and feeling happy about having something besides macaroni and cheese for dinner. I wondered which movies would be in town. With Dad you just have to wait and see what's what. The highway mostly stretched flat like the prairie all around, but every once in a while we'd hit a little hill or slant a little more toward the sun, or away from the sun. I was half hypnotized when we got to this long curve in the road, and that's when we saw it.

Dad slowed down for the curve, so we had a long look at the dog, like a slow-motion video except it's fixed in my brain like no picture I've ever seen. The dog stood in the median strip of dried-up grass, some kind of hound with sad floppy ears, but it had a nose kind of like a deer. It lifted its head like a deer, too. That's when the eyes hit us, kind of half puzzled and half pleading. The eyes said *Help me I don't know what to do.* It held one paw up, like a bird dog on point, but the leg hung a little crooked, maybe hurt, maybe not. Cars whizzed by on either side.

"Dad!"

We were past it now, but there was an exit right up ahead.

He turned his head away. "We can't, son, we've got a full load and it's getting late."

"Dad . . ."

"Traffic's heavy. Just crossing that highway might cause a pile-up. We could get ourselves killed."

I didn't say anymore because my throat was bunched up.

"We'll look on the way back. If he's still there, we'll stop."

The fields blew by without a landmark any-where. How would we know the place? I kept watching for something, anything, that would tell us where we were. Finally the expressway dipped down and the roadside grass ran into some trees, a bridge, a sign. NAMELESS CREEK, it said. Nameless Creek. One of the saddest names I ever heard, like nobody cared enough to call it anything. Like one of Dolly Parton's broken-heart songs. Still, it saved that place from getting lost. Coming back, what we had to do was look for the dog after we passed Nameless Creek.

It seemed like that dog followed me all over the city, watching me unload the truck, pick up the menu, stand in line for the movie, unlock the motel room door. That dog stayed with me all night. When I wasn't thinking about it, I was dreaming about it. The eyes, the paw. It was like I was haunted. My mind twisted around. My sheets twisted around. Dad must have heard me turning over, because all of a sudden, just like we'd come on that dog, his voice sounded out of the dark.

"Son, you're grieving over that dog and you don't even know if it's dead."

"It's lost. If it was dead, that might be better."

Dad was quiet for a while. I thought he had gone

to sleep. Then he said, "Are you talking about that dog or about your mama?"

My throat bunched up again.

"We might never know," he said, "about either one of them."

"Maybe we could have done something."

"About which one?"

"Well, about Mama, something to keep her from leaving. About the dog, something to help it."

"Maybe, if we knew what was the right thing to do. Even if we did the wrong thing, what's done is done."

"But I can't forget it."

"Forgive and forget, that's what they say."

Forgive us our trespasses as we forgive those who trespass against us—that's what we prayed in church. I used to go to church with Mama. It sounded good, that prayer, but they never told you how to forgive.

The next morning we got on the road early. The wind was high and the truck swayed. All Dad's attention was on the steering wheel. We hadn't reached that creek yet, so it was okay. I figured I didn't have to screw up my courage to look until then, or get Dad to think about pulling over. That's why I never found out what happened to the dog. Out of the corner of my eye, some way before we got to the bridge, I caught sight of something brown crumpled up on the median strip. It was something dead, but it could have been anything. How could it be the dog? The dog had been on the other side of Nameless Creek.

After we went over the bridge I looked so hard my eyes burned. But there was nothing in sight except grass on the median strip, nothing beside the road, either. The dog must have made it across the expressway and gone home. It must have had a home. I kept saying that to myself. Dad didn't say anything. He reached over once and wrapped his hand around the back of my neck. Then he gripped the wheel again. I didn't ask him if he'd seen the other thing. Animals get killed on the road all the time, raccoons, deer. It probably wasn't that dog, anyway.

the canine connection

THE LAST THING HELEN remembered seeing was an explosion of red.

The next thing she felt was being pressed down like cloth under a hot iron, the whole world leaning on her body.

"Luke," she said. He had been practicing in the music room, an intricate Mozart concerto that echoed down the parquet hallway hour after hour. He would not quit till he got it right. Yet it was quiet now. Why was this iron pressing on her? She tried to remember past the explosion of red. There had been a crash. Something had fallen off the shelf—the dishes. All the dishes had come crashing down, and the floor had suddenly tilted and slid out from under her feet like she'd seen in a disaster film about a ship at sea, where the dining room piano comes loose during a storm and slides across the floor, crashing into tables full of diners and dishes. But she was not at sea, she was under an iron. She was in their apartment. Her mother was shopping. Her father was at the bank. Her brother was practicing—or not practicing anymore. Perhaps he was thinking about the music, staring out the window the way he did when he needed silence to sort out the sounds. And she had been making sandwiches for them because it was the maid's day off and Luke wouldn't stop to come into the kitchen. He didn't think of lunch unless it appeared in front of him. How was it possible for a twin to be so different, she who sang hit songs with the radio and never missed a meal? Helen hummed a tune she'd heard that morning. It seemed a long time ago and the hum stuck in her throat. She had a terrible headache. Maybe she was dreaming, the nightmare where something's chasing you but you can't move your arms or legs. She could not move anything but her fingers. Then she heard, from far away, some kind of shouting, sirens screaming and screaming. Something shifted over her head and she passed out again.

It was still dark when she woke up and her body

was full of pain. The church bells across the street rang the hour, but she lost count. She could hear a chipping sound, *chink, chink, chink*, like children throwing rocks, and then a dog barking frantically right over her head. Why was a dog barking over her head? She wished it would stop. Every sound felt like a shot. There was a rush of air and suddenly she could breathe more easily and hear the voices of men. She felt something cold and wet on the fingers of her right hand and tried to push it away. Then the iron was taken off her body and she was lifted, very slowly, but it was still too dark to see.

"She's alive," they said. "Get the word to her parents, but tell them she's hurt pretty bad."

"Luke?" she asked. Nobody answered her. They were busy shifting her onto a stretcher and moving her and sticking her with needles. The church bells tolled again, twelve times. It must be midnight, she thought, but she could feel hot sunlight, and then her mind went dark.

She was on a narrow bed and her father was holding her hand. She knew by feeling the carved gold ring on his fourth finger. Someone was crying.

"She's awake, Lillian, I think she's awake."

The crying stopped and the perfume her mother wore floated near. She felt her mother's kiss, her father's kiss, one careful kiss on each cheek, the only places that were not covered with bandage.

"Luke?" she asked. "Where's Luke? What happened?"

It was a long time before she found out. They didn't tell her right away. She picked it up in bits and pieces, like the rubble that was left of their apartment. The earthquake had flattened the building. What saved Helen was a steel beam fallen at an angle that prevented the ceiling from crushing her. No such beam protected Luke. The piano had splintered together with all of his bones.

She thought of the years crushed in that minute, the seventeen years that had already made him famous, the unknown years that would have seasoned him from prodigy to virtuoso to maestro. She thought of the sounds in all the concert halls silenced by crashing dishes. She could think endlessly, but she couldn't cry. Perhaps the bandages that had covered her eyes for so long had sealed the tears. Her mother and father cried, separately and together. She could hear them sometimes at night. They did not cry during the day, for her sake. She could hear them not crying during the day. It must have taken a lot out of them, mourning a dead genius and a blind debutante—blind and, by the feel of her face, scarred despite surgery. She thought of the dress her mother had hidden away in their new apartment. She found it in a box pushed to the back of her closet shelf, surely the same box her mother had carried home on the day of the earthquake, surely a surprise for the eighteenth birthday party concert— the concert for Luke, the party for her. It would be an expensive dress. Money was never an issue. Only perfection. Tall blue-eyed blondes can wear any-thing, her mother used to say, and have all the more reason to define their individual tastes. The dress felt like velvet, black or forest green or dusky rose or wine red. She would never know because she would never ask.

Helen leaned her head back against the armchair in her room and turned off the radio her mother had turned on earlier. She could not bear loud noises. Everything seemed loud to her now. Her parents had dared to buy her a guitar, which stayed quietly in its case. Before the crash she had requested one for her birthday in order to write a song, a song that had circled around in her head for quite a while before she realized it was not from the radio. The song was gone now. She no longer hummed little tunes. She rarely spoke.

"You are isolating yourself," said her mother, but the isolation had begun in the small circle of space that saved her. Her mind stayed in that space though her body had escaped. *I only am escaped alone to tell thee.* A quote from Job in the Bible—she had read that in *Moby Dick* when she could still read.

"You will read again," said her father. He talked about braille and books on tape. Now her parents were talking about a guide dog. "Oh, thanks," said Helen, "the canine connection." It was not as if she had ever relied on friends. She had Luke, or had *had* Luke—past perfect in the grammatical sense, in every sense.

"There's no need to be sarcastic," said her mother softly. "It was a dog that saved you, a search-and-rescue dog."

"I thought the steel beam saved me."

"The dog found you."

Helen remembered a cold, wet touch on the fingers of her right hand. "Maybe he should have left me there."

"Helen! How can you talk like that?"

So she did not talk, not even to the therapist they hired to heal her invisible injuries. More and more she stayed sealed in that circle of space where it was still safe, where Luke reconsidered his interpretation of Mozart while staring out the music room window and her mother shopped for a velvet dress and her father juggled money at the bank. Not that she refused to cooperate. When they insisted on taking her to the Guide Dog Institute, she went. She met her dog and was as polite to him as he was to her.

"We've matched you with a German shepherd," said her trainer, "very handsome, very intelligent." Evidently it was a German shepherd that had found her—not the same one, obviously. She tried to look pleased. The dog's fur was thick and soft. His ears reminded her of velvet. Brown or black velvet, she supposed. When he reached forward for the acquaintance sniff, his cold, wet nose touched the fingers of her right hand, which she pulled back abruptly.

The trainer said nothing for a moment, as if waiting.

"His name is Odin," he said finally. "It's an odd name, but the children in the family who raised him were studying mythology in school. Odin is the Norse god of—"

"I know who Odin is," Helen interrupted. The god of art, culture, war, and the dead. The perfect companion for her.

Helen obediently learned the commands. Odin already knew them, of course, but he practiced with her stoically, tolerant of her mistakes and steadfast in the face of her impatience. She knew the trainer did not like her. His other students were grateful for their dogs. Helen felt nothing except more capable of crossing a street without clinging to her mother's arm. Instead she had to cling to a dog's halter, but at least Odin did not talk. He was a quiet dog and never intruded on her silence. Helen and Odin graduated from the training school and he took up residence in the apartment, where her mother asked her to brush him daily so he would not shed dark fur on the thick new bedroom rug. It was said to be white. Her mother had kept busy redecorating since they moved in. Helen knew this was a model of adjustment. She kept her door closed and, since she gave them no choice, her parents kept their distance.

Odin, too, kept his distance, but it was his own standard of distance, not hers. He stayed exactly close enough to respond as a working dog should when she needed him. There was never any attempt to insinuate himself comfortably on the chair or bed, to impose his head or paw on her lap. He stayed on the floor beside her wherever she was. If she moved, he moved. Without asking, he redrew the circle of space around her to include himself, like a shadow—but too heavy for a shadow. His presence weighed on her, pressed on her heavy as iron. He was not a shadow but a *twin*. She stared sightlessly out the window, unable to move. Of course she walked him dutifully morning, noon, and night. Or did he walk her? She fed him, as the trainer had recommended, feeling her way with the can opener, measuring the dry food from a bag into what smelled like mashed meat, mixing it all together while the maid cleaned the kitchen after her mother's epicurean dinners. Life must go on.

Helen ate very little and she slept less and less, waking often to an explosion of red and a crash of dishes splintering on the tilted floor. Sounds real and imagined made the difference between day and night. This part of town was quiet. She could barely hear the church bells that pealed out every hour across the street from the old apartment. The traffic that passed outside her window was orderly, limited at night to the sibilant motors of homecoming Mercedes, Jaguars, old-fashioned Cadillacs, the occasional Rolls Royce.

Tonight the tires swished gently along the pavement. A scent of spring rain floated through the window toward the bed. Helen heard Odin sigh and felt the press of sleep, heavier, heavier. She was pinned beneath it and could not move. The red exploded again and again like an artery, pumping pain in spurts while cascades of dishes crashed around her, splintering bones and piano keys, and the floor tilted back and forth like a ship on hurricane seas. A siren screamed endlessly into her ears. She felt something cold and wet on the fingers of her right hand. She woke trying to push it away and sat up, but the siren continued screaming and there was another sound beside her rising from low and hollow to higher, ever hollower tones, a black hole of loneliness so unbearable that she could only open her own mouth as the ghost of Luke's Mozart tore loose from her throat and floated upward in a human howl. She could only throw back her head and howl with Odin while the siren screamed past their window. When it faded away their howls died to cries. Runnels of tears ran down her face and neck and nightgown. There was a knock at the door and her mother rushed toward her on a pathway of delicate perfume.

"Helen, are you all right? We heard the most unearthly noise. A siren and . . . I don't know what." Her mother could not see tears in the dark.

Helen dropped her hand to the side of her bed and felt something cold and wet touch her fingers. She smoothed Odin's velvet ears and rested her hand on the strong bones of his head.

"We'll be all right now." She reached out her other hand as her mother turned to go.

"And Mama? Please leave the door open."

the boss

SLY WANTED TO RUN.
Down the hall and out the door, make a clean get-away, they always say that. Wire cages pressed in on him, the whole building was a cage. And it stank. They tried—you could see a guy at the end of one cellblock hosing down the gray cement floor. But there were too many animals, barking, crying, snarling, howling, shitting, pissing, staring at you sad-eyed, or just lying there. That was the worst, the ones with their noses on their paws looking at nothing, not even waiting. Sly passed them by as quickly as he could, but the woman kept stopping, pointing out some dog that would make the best buddy in the

93

world. Sly didn't want a buddy, he wanted a fighter, somebody to guard his ass. He wanted to put this prissy woman on a leash and make her move.

"Look, lady, I told you I want a big dog."

She backed off like he had cooties and looked up at him. "Big dogs are hard to take care of," she said stiffly. "They need a lot of exercise or they'll tear up your house."

"This dog is going to get lots of exercise. Don't you worry about my house." His house, when he went there——the house where his mother lived—— was a dump.

"The next one is big," she said, "part shepherd, very sweet disposition."

Sly shifted his shoulders under the leather jacket and passed on by. Big but old, tired looking. Sly wanted energy. He stopped in front of a massive black dog. When he came closer the dog sank back and raised its lip, just a little bit but you could see a bunch of teeth, like those dinosaur teeth you see on TV.

"This rottweiler just came in, but he's been mistreated. Some neighbor complained. I wouldn't recommend . . . we may have to . . ."

She didn't finish the sentence but she didn't have to. Dead meat. Anyway, he didn't want to get eaten alive, he wanted to stay alive, that's why he was here.

Up ahead there was a kind of strangled banging sound, not as loud as the other racket but steady: *thunk, thunk, thunk.* Sly peered into the cage. *Thunk.* A tight-muscled body hurled itself at the wire. Long legs, lean stomach, skinny tail, all wound up like a spring. *Thunk.*

"Brindle, stop it." *Thunk.* "We call him Brindle because that's the color, sort of speckled like that, but nobody knows his name. They picked him up near some homeless guy who had to go into detox and never came out."

"What kind?"

"The dog?"

"Yeah, the dog." *Not the guy, stupid.*

"It looks like it's got some Staffordshire blood, but don't worry, it's not, well, you know, it's a mixed breed."

"What's wrong with Staffblood?"

"Pit bulls. A lot of people think they can get vicious."

Anything can get vicious, lady. THUNK. This dog didn't look vicious, it looked like it wanted to get out. He could buy that, he wanted to get out too. It was hard to see much more than a blur of short fur, but for a second he caught its eyes. The eyes were yellow with black flecks, sort of the same color as the body but lit up, panicked, like headlights burning holes in the dark.

"This is the one."

"You'd have your hands full, but we can see how you get along with him." She unlocked the cage, eased her hand inside with a short leash, and snapped it on the collar, Collar #1806. The dog's head was pushing on her hand, not looking for a pat or hand-out, looking to get away. His snout found that little space where she'd cracked the door open and he lunged. She barely hung onto him, he was dragging her down the hall toward the windows, her arm sockets popping.

"Whoa," she yelled.

"That ain't no horse, lady, get hold of him."

"I'm trying to," she snapped. "Here, you take him." She unwound the leash, which had wrapped around both her hands, and Sly felt power rocketing through the nylon. He twitched his muscles and gave a little power back, just to show who ruled the powerline.

"This here's a lot of mutt."

"We call them mixed breeds," she said irritably.

He's a mutt, lady, just like the rest of us. Even you.

The dog appeared to be crouching for a leap through the window. Sly jerked him around, and the dog looked up in surprise, as if he'd just realized there was a person there.

"Now, you don't need to manhandle him like

96

that," said the woman. "You'll do better going slow and steady."

Fat lot of good that did you. This ain't no slow steady dog.

The dog was headlighting Sly with his yellow eyes.

Cool it, mutt. Don't mess with me. I am the boss.

"Don't stare into his eyes like that. A lot of dogs take it as a challenge and they'll attack."

Sly turned to stare at her, and she dropped her eyes.

"Okay, let's go into the visiting room for a while," she said. "You two can talk it over and if you agree, we'll sign the papers." She smiled. He did not. She was uneasy about this, but it might be the dog's only chance. Her supervisor was on vacation. She was in charge. The guy was tough but he didn't seem mean, just edgy. There was a difference. She'd seen the difference. He wasn't as old as she'd first thought, and he wasn't rundown or drugged out. He moved like a homegrown athlete, one of those kids who hangs around the playground twenty-four hours a day playing pickup games. It might be a match. "Don't you wish they could tell you where they've been?" she asked, trying to feel him out a little as they walked toward the solid steel door.

No, lady, talking can get you into a lot of trouble.

97

The mutt strained back toward the window but Sly strong-armed him behind the woman's back, and when she opened the door, the mutt shot through it. They both did.

He was a multicultural dog, born half wild on the reservation, taken in by a Mexican family that had to move on fast without him, partial to the homeless black man who fed him for a while, but never counting on handouts. An international dog, too—he raided garbage cans behind Chinese restaurants, Japanese sushi bars, Thai restaurants, Korean diners, French bistros, Irish bars, Italian pizza joints, and the new Jewish deli just transplanted from New York to Arizona. He liked meat but he'd eat anything, and he was too quick to get kicked. You had a sense with this dog that he was always just at the edge of the firelight watching the cavemen roast a carcass, just in case some bone got thrown into the bushes. But he was a lot likelier to catch the bone and run than curl up in the cave. And he wouldn't have told you where he'd been, even if he could have talked, because the habit of silence was deep. He'd seen what happened to dogs that barked and howled all the time. Stealth paid off, he knew that as well as Sly.

It didn't take long for the ASPCA fee to pay off. Sly heard footsteps behind him, keeping pace with his own for a block or so, then starting to close in. They were taking it slow, not sure about the dog. Mutt wasn't fighting to get away, but he wasn't just trotting along nice and easy, either. He was testing the limits of the nylon powerline. Suddenly Sly made a fast turnaround and doubled back. Mutt jumped straight up in the air and spun around like he was shooting a basket. The guys behind them came face to face with a speeding set of canine head-lamps. One pressed over to the wall and scuttled off down the sidewalk. The other took a wide curve into the street to get around them and then kept going. They were vicious, this gang, and they'd been after him for a while. These two would be back with troops, but Sly's mouth twitched. "You gonna play for the Lakers, boy." Mutt glanced up at his voice now, watching for the next move.

His mother's head was slumped over the table and her words were slurred. It didn't matter because whoever she was talking to wasn't there. If she was talking to the bottle, the bottle wasn't listening. It was empty. The whole place was empty. It usually was.

"Where's Day-Glo?"

"He's gone," she mumbled.

"Slinky?"

"Gone. Your sister's gone, your brother's gone, your old man's gone, you're all gone."

"I'm standing right here in front of you."

"Get on out of here."

"I just got back."

"You got nothing."

"I got this dog. And, Ma, I gotta stay here tonight, I gotta buy some time. I gotta get off the street."

She picked up the bottle and smashed it on the floor.

"Gotta, gotta, gotta. You gotta be a crook, go do it, you gotta be a cop, go do it. Go do it and leave me alone."

She was half his size, but she was his mother and she had some kind of powerline, she always had. She looked down at Mutt and back up at Sly, staring at him till he dropped his eyes.

"Out!" She said the one word loud and clear.

He and the dog got out.

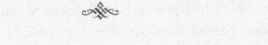

bones

Bones lay in a heap on the floor. He raised his white muzzle toward Mark, gathered his legs under him to lurch upward, and then fell back. His black body settled with a thump. He had been an immense dog, named for the prehistoric bones protruding sometimes out of the blue clay that dropped steeply from their yard to the sea below—Fossil Cliffs. Now his name seemed foreboding. Hidden under handfuls of shaggy fur were only skin and bones. He was an old dog with little muscle or fat to pad the floorboards. Mark and his mother Nell watched him give way and they watched each other. Neither spoke, but they both remembered.

Nell had just turned eighteen when she missed one period, then another. She bought a drugstore testing kit, which confirmed that she was pregnant. She had not studied biology and chemistry for nothing. Or maybe she hadn't studied them enough. Her boyfriend gave her money for an abortion and then transferred to another school at midterm. Nell never saw him again. On the morning of her appointment she sat in the waiting room of the clinic and watched the other young women. Some were alone, some not. Some were openly nervous, others masking it. Each harbored a cluster of busily multiplying cells in her uterus. Nell thought about cells, some becoming nerves, some blood, others bone. She thought of her father, alone in his house on Fossil Cliffs, a cluster of ailing nerves, blood, and bone. Then she looked down at her own trim young body, walked to the desk, cancelled the appointment, and called her father from a pay phone.

From that moment her life proceeded like tides on the shore. She lived by lists of things to do and often found that her class papers were filled with sentences consisting of series, like ocean waves. Nell calculated her due date, finished the semester with straight A's, and then went home. It took two more years to get her Bachelor of Science degree, commuting to the local state university program, caring for Mark after he was born, and nursing her father while he died of cancer. They were hard years patched together with student loans, baby-sitters, and home-care helpers. Mark lent a joyful rhythm to their lives. Sleeping and waking he thrived, reminding them that the world at large renews itself each morning and rests itself at night.

The summer after she graduated, when Mark was two years old, Nell's father died. He was Mark's only other relative and Nell felt the need of some other continuity in their lives. There wasn't much money after the medical and funeral bills were paid, but she had the house in Fossil Cliffs and her job in a hospital laboratory. After the funeral she located a breeder of Newfoundland dogs and bought the biggest puppy in his latest litter. Baby-sitters might come and go, a grandfather might disappear, a mother might leave for work, but a dog was full-time.

Mark was a sturdy boy but Bones quickly outweighed him. While Mom talked about fond memories of Grandpa Mark, young Mark's memories mostly had to do with a warm mountain of black fur, very sloppy kisses after every meal, and a stubborn wall between him and the ocean. "Shore patrol," Mom would say to Bones, and unless she called him off, the dog would block Mark from going into the sea on their daily walks along the beach. Depending on the season Mark and Bones and Mom often had the whole beach to themselves. Most of the houses on Fossil Cliffs were summer cabins, not insulated against the hungry storms that ate at the cliffs during late autumn, winter, and early spring. It was after such storms that Mark and Mom would sometimes see bones sticking out of the blue clay of the cliffs and would call Mom's friends in Zoology. Mostly they found sharks' teeth on the dark, silty sand below the cliffs. There seemed to be an endless shedding of these teeth from primordial jaws embedded under the sands of the sea. They ranged from needle-like to a foot long. Grandpa Mark had found a few big ones, over the decades, and propped them up on the fireplace mantel. Mean teeth, Mark called them. He longed to find a mean tooth himself and filled jars with small curving gray ones in the process of building his collection of fossils.

Bones did not have much patience for scientific investigation. He preferred barking at crabs, digging holes in the sand with his gigantic paws, and plunging into the surf after sticks of driftwood thrown by anyone he could beg to do it. Usually this meant only Mark or Mom, since the average sunbather avoided a 150-pound dog that drooled copiously and sprayed sheets of water some distance away during a brisk shake. Squeamish visitors tended to avoid their beach, anyway, because of the jellyfish that could sting a swimmer or simply squish underfoot between the black rocks littering the sand. Bones did not seem to mind jellyfish, dead or alive, though they were one of the few items that he did not eat.

"We should have called him Teeth," said Mom, pulling him away from a fish that was several days dead.

"Or maybe Jaws," said Mark.

Mom laughed and threw a hunk of driftwood into the sea.

By the time Mark turned nine, he was allowed to roam the beach alone, so long as he followed three strict rules: He had to tell Mom or the after-school sitter where he was going; he could never swim alone without human adult supervision; and he had to be home before dark. Mark always followed these rules, and Bones always followed Mark. The only time they broke the rules was accidental and nearly fatal.

It was an unusually warm Saturday in October and Mom was home but busy with weekend chores. Mark and Bones had walked farther southward than usual. They stopped to rest in a sheltered niche. The base of the cliffs cut off the wind but allowed the sun to bake them. Curled up together in a clump of sandy fur and damp jacket, they both drifted off to sleep. Mark woke to the bellow of Bones's barking. The dog stood over him stiff legged and anxious, circling away and then running back to bark again. When Mark sat up and looked around, he saw that they were surrounded behind and ahead by the incoming tide. Their niche was an island that would soon sink underwater. The sky had dulled to gray and the wind had picked up, slamming waves against the base of the cliffs wherever the beach narrowed close to the sea. Mark turned toward home and watched as the surf in front of him sucked back and pitched forward, blocking his path. There was no way up the cliffs except for the steep steps built from their own beach far ahead. They had to get through this roiling stretch of water to the broader beach beyond.

It was too far to run between waves. If he could just make it to one of the higher rocks along the way, maybe he could hold on through a wave and get the rest of the way before another crashed. Bones was faster and stronger. Bones could make it in one run. When the next wave crashed and began to pull back, Mark called, "Go, Bones" and charged into the water as close to the cliff base as he could. The blue clay was slippery and his feet slid out from under him. It was not the pushing but the pulling that took him. He had underestimated the power of the suction drawing him away. On his hands and knees, clawing at blue clay and rocks, he was caught by the next wave thundering over his head. He could feel his body whipping away. He struggled to breathe, to keep his head up. Salt water filled his nose and throat. His feet brushed the bottom once or twice, but he was the ocean's bait, dangled near the rocks, pulled away, and thrown back against them, hard. An omnivorous ocean waited to swallow him.

Salt-choked, he lunged with all his might, scrabbling at the slick rocks, felt them sharp against his arm, *around* his arm—*teeth,* he was being pulled by teeth. For an instant he saw himself towed away in the grip of sharks' teeth, in payment for all those he'd taken from the sea. Then a wall rose between him and the open ocean, something sodden and strong swam beside him, not a shark. He clung to it, churning his other arm as hard as he could, pushing forward, gaining way. Water pulled slowly lower at his body, from neck to chest to hips to thighs to knees to ankles and he was free, throwing himself forward on the sand in a shaken, aching heap with a giant black dog sluicing off sheets of water beside him. Bones nuzzled his ear and neck until Mark finally gathered himself together and stumbled toward home, a drizzle of rain spitting at him from the Atlantic.

"He saved my life, you know, that time we got caught in the tide."

"I know."

"We can't just do nothing, Mom."

"We've done all we can, except for the surgery."

"The vet says the surgery might give him some time."

"What kind of time, Mark? He's an old dog."

"Only fourteen."

"That's old for a big dog, and there comes a point where . . ."

Her voice trailed off.

"Where what?"

"There are worse things than dying."

"But the vet said . . ."

"That's the vet's job."

"Are you saying he just wants the money?"

"Maybe he just wants to win."

"He did say the surgery might not work."

"Yes, he was honest about that. But he didn't mention the trauma of surgery on an old dog even if he survives it. And he doesn't know the way this dog cries at the door when you walk to the beach alone because he can't go up and down those stairs anymore. His body is closing down, Mark, this is a whole process, it's not just one thing. He's been peeing all over the house . . ."

"I clean that up."

"I'm not talking about the mess, I'm talking about the organism, the bladder, the cataracts—he's nearly blind now—the arthritis, the cancer . . ."

"Like Grandpa Mark."

"All right, yes."

"Would you have put Grandpa Mark out of his misery?"

There was a long pause.

"He wanted me to."

"But you didn't, did you? And Bones can't talk, so we don't know what he wants."

"He'll tell us, Mark, if we listen."

Mom got up from the couch and left the room. She was sad, Mark knew, and angry—angry at him, at Bones, at Grandpa Mark, at herself. She had said this before, how one death raises the pain of others. Mark's head ached, his thoughts at war, pounding first in one direction, then another, fighting every step of the way. He got up from the couch and lay down beside Bones. The old dog lifted his head for a moment and then laid it down. Mark put his arm around him and his own head on the soft black fur and heard the heartbeat thumping, thumping, thumping under the bones. It sounded like waves of the sea, waves of the sea that come in and must then, he knew, go out.

afterword

WRITING A STORY INVOLVES two kinds of experience, the factual and the imagined. One is no less real than the other and no less authentic when realized as fiction. Each of the stories in this collection has a different ratio of factual and imagined experience. All of them include something that actually happened or existed—an incident, a place, a person, an animal, a feeling—and much that was invented. Two of the stories, "Cargo" and "A Grave Situation," grew out of newspaper reports that appeared, respectively, in *The Washington Post* (thanks to Don Phillips) and "Earthweek: A Diary of the Planet," Steve Newman's syndicated column. For those curious about where writers get their ideas, these two examples show how a factual story can grow into a fictional story that retains some common truth while diverging completely in details and development.

The other stories are variously rooted in personal experience: "Lab," on attending the birth of my first grandchild; "Restaurant," in two separate scenes I witnessed on the northern Italian coast, neither involving romance; "Room 313," on the pure-hearted benevolence of a physical therapist's pet; "The Drive," on my own fight against impatience during excursions with my elderly mother; "Fiona and Tim," on my involvement with Irish Border collies; "The Nose," on certain affinities for garbage that I've noticed in children and dogs; "Nameless Creek," on a trip I took with one of my daughters; "The Canine Connection," on an atavistic, irresistible urge to join my dogs when they howl; "The Boss," on a difficult canine personality I observed in training sessions; and "Bones," on the part of Chesapeake Bay where I paid childhood visits to my uncle. These bits and pieces of personal experience become part of the puzzle that fits together with purely imagined chunks of character, plot, setting, and image for a complete story. Once I have the emotional core, the story seems to write itself, with details appearing unexpectedly on the page as I write. This creative process requires steady practice and great faith in subconscious connections.

If there is a theme to the whole collection, it is one that I did not recognize till afterwards—that animals and young humans share a heart-wrenching vulnerability which makes them empathetic metaphors for one another. From the beginning, I did have a goal for the collection—to include the variety of tone and situation I enjoy reading myself, ranging from a humorous spoof like "The Nose" to the tension in "Cargo" and the tears I shed over

"Bones." My goal for any short story is to leave a reader satisfied with the brief experience of a whole world. The short stories that I have not liked in my reading and writing life have been those that did not enclose me completely. Yet there is always a complex balance involved in selecting what's essential to include and exclude. Paradoxically, a good story—whether long or short—leaves one both satisfied and wanting more.

J. R. R. Tolkien's book *The Hobbit* is subtitled "There and Back Again," a deceptively simple phrase that summarizes all stories, from the briefest folktale to the realistic novel or the multivolume fantasy series. For the reader to journey, the writer must do so first, with the same intensity that she hopes the reader will experience. There are no shortcuts for either, but in a world where lack of time and attention is epidemic, the short story fits naturally as a journey there and back again.

about the author

BETSY HEARNE is the author of several books for children, including *Wishes, Kisses, and Pigs* (a *Child* magazine Best Book of 2001), *Eliza's Dog,* and *Listening for Leroy* (a Notable Social Studies Trade Book for Young Children). She was formerly the editor of the *Bulletin of the Center for Children's Books,* and she now teaches literature and storytelling at the University of Illinois in Urbana-Champaign. Ms. Hearne lives with her family in Urbana, Illinois.